Faster Pussycats

Faster Pussycats

LIVE GIRLS: AFTER HOURS

edited by Trixi

alyson books
los angeles | new york

MANUFACTURED IN THE UNITED STATES OF AMERICA.

THIS TRADE PAPERBACK ORIGINAL IS PUBLISHED BY
ALYSON PUBLICATIONS,
P.O. BOX 4371, LOS ANGELES, CA 90078-4371.
DISTRIBUTION IN THE UNITED KINGDOM BY
TURNAROUND PUBLISHER SERVICES LTD.,
UNIT 3, OLYMPIA TRADING ESTATE, COBURG ROAD, WOOD GREEN,
LONDON N22 6TZ ENGLAND.

FIRST EDITION: AUGUST 2001

01 02 03 04 05 **a** 10 9 8 7 6 5 4 3 2 1

ISBN: 1-55583-587-2

LIBRARY OF CONGRESS CATALOGING-IN-PUBLICATION DATA
FASTER PUSSYCATS: LIVE GIRLS : AFTER HOURS / EDITED BY TRIXI.
ISBN 1-55583-587-2
1. LESBIANS—SEXUAL BEHAVIOR. I. TRIXI.
HQ75.5.F37 2001
306.76'63—DC21   2001023988

CREDITS
COVER DESIGN BY MATT SAMS.
COVER PHOTOGRAPHY BY TINA TYRELL.

Contents

Introduction

About a year and a half ago, Buck, my tube sock–donning, boy porn–directing friend, and I were sucking down drops of lemon and fingers of whiskey at a local watering hole when we got on to the feisty topic of dyke print-porno and what appealed to us. Then, of course, we debated until we agreed who "us" is; we are "queers with an urban aesthetic" (damn it). Hey, it was midnight, and Johnnie Walker thought the definition was *fabulous*.

The nuance of the current dyke is subtle—it's about experimenting with S/M without joining a group, about being butch when you're topped, about shaving your head so you can wear wigs, about piercing and poking what is mutually agreed upon without apology, about stage dives and homemade soaps and makeup and men's shoes—*simultaneously*. Or, as my amazing new wife, Crystal, put it, "It doesn't matter anymore—it's just all about boning." She'll be a street poet yet.

For *Faster Pussycats,* I decided to give boundary to the boning—all the action must be *real* and take place in queer dance clubs, strip joints, bars, or sex clubs. With that in mind, I sent out the call for submissions and within two months found myself buried under stacks of wonderfully tawdry true-life stories. From these I chose only the finest naughtiness representing spots all over the physical and sexual map: *On Our Backs* editor and sex educator extraordinaire Tristan Taormino tells us about her first professional dominatrix experience; a pair of drag kings shows the leather daddies how it's done; a woman describes the ritual of a final fling in "Last Tango in Paris, Texas"; an expatriate loses her virginity after a night in a South Korean dyke bar; two liquored-up lassies let it all go in a public bathroom; and a jet-setter partakes in some hot club action in Amsterdam with a feisty local. But wait, there's more: bare-assed lawyers in a Canadian sex club, chicks with strap-ons, waifish goths, lap dances, and, of course, Vegas. I'm certain there will be at least one scenario in *Faster Pussycats* you've wanted to do but never have, whether it's earning a slave's collar or ending the night with an innocent kiss.

All said, I'd like to thank Angela Brown for her patient and brilliant assistance, all the authors for their wonderful contributions, Buck for suggesting the book's title, and my wifey for being, well, my wifey.

—Trixi
Los Angeles, 2001

Virgins & Good Girls

No Time for Prayers

ALMA VADA

"Sorry to be dressed in full clerical drag, but I had to come straight from church. Things are so hectic right now. The rector left me in charge while he's on a three-month sabbatical." Janet was standing on the front porch, dressed in her black shirt and white collar, an ornate silver cross hanging around her neck.

"You know I love a woman in drag," I laughed. "Come on in. I'm just making the pasta. I meant to have this done before you came, but it'll just take a minute. I'm making a cream sauce with poached salmon. Think I should put dill in the pasta dough?"

"Mmm. Sounds great. What are those shapes?"

"Rotini. Kinky pasta. But they don't seem to be twisting much." While I pulled off the little bits of pasta coming out of the machine, Janet opened the bottle of cabernet sauvignon she had brought for herself. Although I had given up drinking years ago, the aroma was tantalizing.

I slipped the pasta off the plate into the boiling water. "There. So tell me what's going on at church."

Janet and I had been buddies for 20 years, but she had joined the clergy full-time three years earlier, after a more debauched younger life. We had remained close friends through all these permutations, through tragedies and several changes of lovers.

"He left me in charge, and good God Almighty, what a headache," she said. "But the real big blowup has to do with these queens who want a marriage ceremony. The rector just dumped this controversy in my lap as he was leaving. And let me tell you, nothing's worse than a queen with her panties in a twist."

"How old's the rector?"

"Fifty. Why?"

"I thought you might be next in the line of succession."

"God save me from that. I don't enjoy balancing books or balancing people. The little old ladies with their altar society and their flower guild. I mean, is it my mission to deal with the people who didn't like the flowers last Sunday? I much prefer to spend my time ministering to the homeless and the perverts at the transient hotels, especially the pre-op transsexuals."

I drained the cooked pasta, and steam surged from the sink, up over my face. I arranged the poached salmon over the plates of pasta, then poured the cream sauce on top of the arrangement. We sat down at the table, which I had covered with a multitude of little squashes in orange, green, and white, accented with a simple vase of crimson Japanese maple leaves. The low lights of skinny green tapers and fat purple candles flickered softly in the midst of it all.

"Everything is so beautiful…and delicious," Janet said as she tasted the first bite of pasta.

"Thank you." I passed the silky salmon between my lips, savoring the delicate texture.

"I went to see a dominatrix," Janet said, out of the blue.

"Oh, God! I need the details." While we had shared confidences over the years, this was something new.

"You always have needed the details. You're a bona fide cross-examiner!"

"Start from the beginning. How did you find her?"

"On the Internet."

"Like what, in a chat room?"

"No…" Janet paused. "She had a Web page."

"A Web page. Oh, stop! How do you find a Web page like that?"

"Just like any other search. You know, you enter a topic and do a search."

"What topic do you use to look for a dominatrix?"

"So many questions!" Janet fluttered her fingers in front of her face, then blushed a little. "*Submission* is one of the words. Things like that, yeah." She took a long sip of the crimson wine.

Submission. I rolled the word around in my mind, moved the pasta through the cream sauce, twisted around in my chair. I looked up at Janet, who was by now looking back at me, unblinking. She moved a wisp of her light brown hair off her forehead.

"And then?"

"I E-mailed her and she E-mailed me back. Then I went up to see her in Fennimore Park."

"Tell me everything about the first time you saw her."

"She asked me to wear my clerical garb."

"Wait, wait. She knew you were in the clergy?"

"I had told her about it in the E-mails. I waited until I was at her door and then quickly stuck the collar on. That's all I needed, to be parading around like that. She's French, raised in Paris, went to church at Notre Dame, so she's crazy for the whole priest part of it. She told me to wear my pajamas, so after

I was inside I put on the red flannel pajamas I brought."

"Red flannel pajamas? You were in your pajamas?" I was trying to evoke the scene of Janet in red pajamas with the dominatrix; the pajamas mystified me, but there was so much more to ask. "Did she have a dungeon?"

"Yes. She took me out to a separate building, about the size of this dining room. It had every kind of device. A hanging rack full of different whips—thin ones, big ones. Restraints. Leather gear. Masks of various kinds. Actually tasteful; you'd like her decorating touch. One of the best things she had was this little wooden paddle. She was unsure at first, said she didn't know me very well, and didn't know whether it would offend me or not. A little wooden paddle with the words JESUS LOVES YOU on it."

We howled in unison.

"Oh, God, it's too funny." I was still laughing.

A new CD started playing. "I hope you don't mind Vivaldi," I said. "I haven't listened to *The Four Seasons* in ages."

"I like Vivaldi. It has the comfort of an old friend—it's so familiar."

"Now back to your dominatrix."

"My favorite was when we played shoe store. I loved it. She pulled out all these pairs of black high heels and made me arrange them in order of most to least used. I had to smell them to determine how used they were. Then I tried the shoes on her. As I tried on the shoes, I had to adjust them, make sure her feet were comfortable, adjust her stockings up to her thighs. I ran my hands up to where the stockings ended, mid thigh, and the bare flesh began beneath her garters. Then she paraded back and forth in the shoes. She asked me where I would have her wear each pair. To the opera, the theater, the office. I've always loved women's shoes. When I was a kid I used to go into my mother's closet and smell her shoes. It was a fantasy growing up—being a shoe salesperson and having women thrust their bare feet between my open legs."

"Deacon Janet!" I exclaimed. "I've never heard this from you. All these years I've known you, I had no idea you had a little shoe fetish."

"After the shoe store game she spanked me," Janet continued, undaunted. "When she had warmed my butt she flipped me over and jammed her knee into my crotch. I exploded into an orgasm immediately. Then she masturbated on my leg. Later she said the whole episode was kind of unusual for her, and she didn't charge me."

My breathing was laden and measured, and I was suddenly very aware of it. I licked the last of the cream sauce off my fork. I looked into Janet's face, a face I had never considered sexually before, and noticed anew how beautiful her brown eyes were, how sensual her small pink lips appeared.

"Do you think less of me?" Janet looked at me earnestly.

"Oh, please. You're kidding—why would I? Has anyone else said anything negative?"

"Now you're kidding. I couldn't tell anyone but you."

"I think it's perfect for you. Just what you want. And it's contained and hassle-free."

"Exactly. There's no negotiation. None of this, 'If I do this for you, then you'll have to do this for me.' And no judgment. Then I can go home to the cat afterward and sleep alone, which is what I really prefer."

"But the important question is: How do you feel about it?"

"I'm trying to figure it out. Did I have sex with her? Does that mean I went to a prostitute?"

"But you didn't pay."

"That makes it simple, doesn't it?" she asked, mildly sarcastic.

"And so what if you did? I used to think it would be so simple if there were really hot lesbian prostitutes, because too many lesbians are way low on the sex thermometer."

"Isn't that the truth!"

I stood and picked up our plates. "Are you ready to cool down a bit? I made pomegranate sorbet."

"I'd love some, thank you. So…who are you fucking?"

"Fucking? What's that? It's been so long. No one."

"No one! I can't believe that," Janet said. "How's the school-teacher? Still seeing Tatia?"

"I told you she's leaving the country. Without me. Haven't seen her for weeks."

"What's going on with you two?

"Now, nothing. But when we were together, we had the best sex ever."

"Ever?"

"Ever. When we went to Thailand she was a different girl in every town. She brought exotic attire for each place. In Bangkok she was a whore in red silk, a beach girl in a tropical print in the islands, a lacy Victorian in Chang Mai, where we had a four-poster bed. At the Oriental Hotel, when we came back to Bangkok, she had an elegant black outfit. She planned this in advance and surprised me on the trip. She loved fantasy, loved play. And she knew how to be obedient." I connected with Janet's eyes as I underscored the last word.

"You always said you had a good time with her." Janet leaned forward. "Tell me, in all your travels, have you ever been to a sex professional?"

I hesitated. "Did I ever tell you about Java?"

"I don't think so," Janet said.

"Look, I'm going to tell you everything, things I've never told anyone else."

Janet had the slightest smile on her face.

"I had gone to New Guinea with Rosie, long after we were lovers, to the Indonesian side called Irian Jaya."

"I remember when you went," Janet said.

"It had taken us days to get to the highlands because of how inaccessible it is. It was our first day there, and we had hooked up with a local guide. We were all having lunch at a small place, eating river fish that tasted like mud, when the woman who ran the place started massaging my shoulders. She had great hands, and I asked her if I could get a massage later. 'Sure,' she told me. 'Come back after dinner.' So I went back after dinner."

"Where was Rosie?" Janet asked.

"She stayed at the rooming house. I went by myself. The woman I'd met at lunch led me back behind the kitchen, down a hallway, into a tiny room that looked like someone's bedroom. It was dark by then, and the warm light of a kerosene lamp flickered on the wooden walls of the room. There was a small bed, taking up almost the whole room."

"Sounds a little strange." Janet's brows were knitted.

"It got stranger," I continued. "There was this tiny desiccated old crone standing by the bed, dressed in an aged brown sarong, with her straight gray hair pulled back into a bun at the nape of her neck. The woman from the restaurant told me the old lady would be giving me the massage, not her. I stared at the old woman, who must have weighed less than 90 pounds. 'Really, she's much better,' the woman assured me."

"What did you do? Weren't you a little concerned?" Janet asked.

"I was dubious but thought, heck, I'm here. The old woman and I were left alone, and she motioned for me to take off my clothes and lie on the bed, which I did. As soon as she touched me, I knew she was strong and skillful. She went for my sensitive points and worked them. Before long she was pressing on a point on my inner thigh that really turned me on."

"My word!" Janet's eyes widened and glistened.

"I felt the pressure going straight to my clit, as if she were touching me there directly. I glanced at the old woman, but she didn't betray anything; there was no smirk, no smile, no glimmer that showed she was doing this deliberately."

I stopped to catch my breath, then went on. "I was getting

more and more excited, and I wanted her to continue. I felt my muscles tensing as the pleasure mounted. At the same time a part of me was looking down on this scene and thinking, *Whoa! What's going on?!* I mean, here I was, in a remote land, inhabited by locals who walked around town naked and supposedly still practiced cannibalism. I was alone, lying naked in the back of ramshackle building, with an old woman I didn't know stimulating me sexually, and I was sure she was doing it deliberately. But she kept working on me, and I wanted it. She kept pressing, pressing, and I was just getting hotter and hotter, until she got me so excited that I came."

"What did she do then?" Janet asked.

"She didn't say anything; in fact, she didn't speak any English at all. And she didn't act as if anything had happened. I turned over onto my stomach, and she worked on my back. I realized it was getting late and that I should get back to my rooming house and to Rosie. I left the old woman a generous tip, which she accepted without a word; her eyes didn't even meet mine."

As I finished my tale, a thick, almost muggy, awkward silence held everything together. Our eyes flicked across each other's face and away.

Janet broke the silence. "I should be going. Excuse me, I'll just go to the bathroom first."

I told her to go on, that I would clear the table. I corked the remaining wine, inhaling its perfume one last time. As I was putting the bottle into the bag, Janet came up behind me, very near, and breathed into my ear, "If you weren't such a dear old friend, I'd fuck your brains out right now."

I turned, smiled up into Janet's face, and pressed my parted lips against hers. Janet's hands ran over me, softly but hungrily, touching my ass, my thighs, squeezing my now erect nipples. Our bodies rubbed against each other.

"Oh, God, what…" A moment's hesitation about changing

our platonic relationship washed over me and evaporated in the heat.

"Let's go up to your bedroom," Janet murmured.

Things were tossed off the bed, where no company had been expected. Janet turned off the table lamp, leaving a trickle of light from the hall.

We immediately fell onto the bed. I hiked her legs over my shoulders and thrust my pelvis into her still-clothed crotch over and over, pressing into her warm and wet center. Janet's head went back under the pillows, and her hands clenched at her cheeks. Then she went slack as I lay on top of her. She sat up after a minute and took off my shirt and bra. I stripped her black shirt and white collar off. In the chaos of our undressing each other, she reached for my naked breast.

"Pinch my nipples," I instructed. "Harder. Really hard. Yeah, like that. And when you suck, bite a little. Yes, yes." She was a quick pupil. "And what do you like?" I asked her.

"I like it up the ass," she said huskily.

I reached under the bed, and brought out a box of tiny latex circles and a tube of K-Y.

"What are those?" Janet asked.

"Finger cots, condoms for fingers—you know, safe sex and all."

I twisted the top off the little vial of lubricant and let it gush down the crack of her ass. My finger wiped around in the slippery goo until I found her puckered little anus and thrust into her. Janet's muscles gripped my finger, and she groaned, "Yes, fuck me."

My finger slid along the silky smooth track, back and forth over the little ridge inside, sending shivers into Janet, filling her. In and out I slid until she cried out and I felt her muscles' grip on my finger relax. As I pulled out, her whole body relaxed. Her breathing was deep and steady as she rolled over, her eyes sparkling in the dim room.

"Did you leave me any lube?" she asked. Janet's thumb went

inside my ass. "You like everything at once, don't you?" she said as she stuffed her fingers inside my cunt and slid along my clitoris with another finger. How could she know this? I was thrilled, with an incredible satisfaction from being so completely filled; I was out of my mind. She increased her rhythmic movements until I went over the top, coming in waves.

"I could fuck you like this all night," Janet muttered into my ear from behind me.

And I could have let her.

It was heaven. She was heavenly.

I turned to my pupil. "OK, now you have been naughty, naughty. You think you can just come over here and seduce me like this?"

"Apparently," Janet laughed, which made me laugh and fall momentarily out of my role.

"Now your punishment will be even worse, because you are disrespectful as well." I rummaged through a basket in my closet and brought out a long black leather strap. I snapped it, which brought Janet to attention.

"What are you doing?"

"Whatever I want. Turn over on your stomach," I commanded. She obeyed, and I slapped the strap against her rear.

Janet's head jerked, but she didn't resist, so I spread her legs and slapped between her legs with the strap, again and again until even in the dim light it was apparent that she was red and warm.

I mounted Janet's ass and slithered up and down, my cunt juicy from administering punishment. The frenzy spread through me, up through my head, and I cried out, arched my back, and slumped across Janet's back, moaning.

I rolled off Janet and onto the bed, still moaning, off somewhere. Janet cradled me, stroking my sweaty forehead, kissing my cheek.

My panting and moaning eventually subsided and I turned to Janet.

"Did you make it up?"

"What?"

"The story about the dominatrix. Is it true?"

"Hmm." She looked at me. "Does it matter?"

Lipstick Boy

KRISTEN E. PORTER

Provincetown. My birthday. Friends. What could be better? We are at the club—the only lesbian club in the area, which is strange for such a gay town. I dance a bit by myself and am furious to find out that during my jaunt to the dance floor my friends decided to go back to the hotel. I sit myself down, waiting for the clock to strike midnight and have my 28th year finally be over. Tick. Tock. Twelve. I'm overwhelmed that here I am, it's my birthday, and no one is here to celebrate with me.

I begin to think about my ex-lover who was supposed to be here. We just broke up a few days ago, and I told her not to come. It isn't unusual for me to be alone. Nor is it unusual for me to be forgotten about. My thoughts ride quickly down, spiraling into a sea of self-defeating feelings. 12:10 A.M.…still my birthday…still sitting at the club. Tears roll down my face.

Maybe people will think they're just drops of sweat from dancing, or maybe no one will notice in this dimly lit bar. Jesus, I told myself this year would be better. Saturn is supposedly outta my damn sign. I can't believe they left. Before midnight, even! This sucks. What am I supposed to do? I've gotta just let go and move on. I can still have fun by myself.

With that thought, I glance over to the bar and spot a delicious woman walking by. Our eyes meet. She smiles, and perhaps with one too many cosmopolitans, I blurt out, "It's my birthday!" She saunters over, wearing a burgundy lace slip and leopard-print jacket. She is an exotic beauty, a goddess appearing from nowhere. Her skin is a translucent olive color, and right between her eyebrows sparkles a deep red jewel of some sort. Not a real one, but one of those trendy stick-ons.

With a sexy smoker's voice, she says, "How 'bout a birthday kiss?" Her eyes are like a Persian cat's and burn right through me. She leans over and puts her lips against mine. Soft and strong. Her tongue darts for mine.

We kiss deeply for what feels like a few minutes. The space between my legs throbs, and my hunger for her melts into a wetness I haven't felt during a kiss in a long time. With my arm around her waist, I feel the strings of her thong, the curve of her hips.

Is this really happening? Is it really happening to me? Shit, I wish I could stop thinking and just kiss her. Just enjoy her.

The club lights turn up, and in their fluorescent horror her crimson stain appears all over my face. She grabs some bar napkins and wipes my face.

Leave your stain on me so I'll have a memory of your gift. I don't care if your lipstick stays on my face forever. I am in awe of you, the situation. I am immersed in a fantasy I can't even imagine, let alone believe, is happening right here, right now, to me.

"Do you want to get a slice of pizza?" she asks.

"Yeah, sure," I answer, thinking I never want tonight to end.

We sit on the sidewalk eating our slices, watching the people pass by, chatting. Silly talk. Friend talk. Sex talk. Drunk talk.

"What's your name?" I wonder if this will ruin the mystery and magic.

"Asia," she replies.

Like the continent, I assume, although I'm not sure I heard her correctly. "I've traveled all over Europe, the U.S., and Asia, and picked that up as my name. I think I'm off next to the Islands. I want to open up a bed-and-breakfast there."

"Wow. That's adventurous. How do you support yourself along the way?"

"I go to a place, stay for a while, strip until I save up enough money, and move on. I live in my van with my dog."

This all sounds too bizarre. Maybe she's a struggling actress and is trying out a new role on me? Maybe she's a pathological liar? A scam artist? Maybe she is a stripper named Asia who lives in a van and travels around the world with her dog. I can hear my friend Michael's voice: *Leave it to you to pick up the homeless for your birthday!*

I chuckle to myself.

"What are you laughing about?" she asks.

"Oh, just how strange this all is."

"Let's go back to my van. I have to let the dog out."

Well, here we are. The van does exist. It's probably a 1990 model. The burgundy paint clashes with the orange rust spots. The windows are covered with material so I can't see in from the outside. She opens the door, and the inside drips with silks and velvets. Purples, blacks, crimsons, and forest greens fill my vision. Rich, deep colors. The kind of colors you would see in a Victorian tapestry. The backseats of the van are folded down, and a futon mattress lies on them, covered with a patchwork quilt. Seeing me look at it, she says, "I made that from old skirts and dresses."

Seems like Stevie Nicks should be singing "Gypsy" in the background.

Out pops the dog, a Chihuahua named Lipstick Boy. I climb in and try to make myself comfortable while she walks him.

A dog. Cute. Not really. I don't like dogs. But I'd better pretend to. Dykes and their dogs, you know. Hope he doesn't jump all over me. I hope I don't have to let him lick my face.

When she returns to the van, she falls into my arms on the mattress. Her full lips are on mine with a fierceness that instantly makes me hot. Our tongues dance so well together, no awkward steps, no tripping over each other's feet. Her body melts into mine. Her softness eases the rigidity of my body. My hipbones get lost in her roundness.

I can't wait to get this slip thing off her. Up over the head, that's it. Her breasts are toppling out of her black lace bra like gourds in a cornucopia. Oh, they feel so good as she rubs them lightly across my own. Is this a front or back closure? Back, good. Off with the bra. She must have already taken off her G-string. The pressure of her tits against mine makes my nipples feel as if they could explode through my tank top. Please touch them. Bite them. Something. A pinch, even.

Right to business for Asia. She climbs off me and kneels on the floor of the van. "Do you mind if I fuck you with my strap-on?"

"Uh, sure, as long as you have a condom for it."

God, sometimes I sound so stupid. Why couldn't I have come up with something cute and witty like, "Sure, slip into something more erect"? She's so forward…perhaps she's the town slut and this is a nightly routine for her. And for me, it's just another birthday.

She pulls from under her bed a leather harness and marbleized dildo. She suits up.

Kristen E. Porter

Oh, jeez, she's opening the condom package with her teeth. Staring at me with those kohl-smudged almond eyes. Tiger eyes.

She rolls the rubber down her erection. I turn over on my stomach, my ass in the air, as she comes from behind and teases my cunt with her silicone. I slide myself back onto her cock, my hands reaching behind to her thighs, and pull her close to me. She begins to fuck me with the rhythm of an African drummer.

I'm so glad I don't need any lube. I'm wet. Dripping wet. One thing I don't need to be embarrassed about. Thank God I don't have any zits on my ass.

I lean onto my elbows and move my hand to my already swollen clit. I step up the tempo of my vibrating fingers.

Oh, yeah, this feels too good. I wonder what it looks like from her view. My alabaster ass in the air. Her dildo fucking deep within me. I want to feel her. Does this turn her on? Are juices dripping from her velvety lips?

I take my hand and reach for her, but she grabs my arm and stops me. "No, you can't do that. You were just touching yourself. It's not safe."

God, she's right. I feel stupid for being scolded. I should've thought about that. It's been so long since I've been with someone other than my ex-lover. I feel naive again.

I go back to playing with myself. The tension starts to build. Our angles are perfect. I can feel her rubbing against my sweet spot.

God, let me come. Please. I know I had a lot to drink tonight. If you let me come, I'll never drink this much again. Promise. This night is too perfect to fake it. Shit. OK, relax. Stop praying and enjoy. It's starting to build.

My hand is getting tired, so I switch from circles to side to side. Close. Very close. She reaches her hands around and grabs hold of my tits. She squeezes my nipples hard in her fingers, and before I even know what's happening, my back arches uncontrollably, and a wave of pleasure comes over me. She's still fucking me, and I ride the waves.

Was that scream from me? Was it out loud?

I collapse onto the bed, her on top of me. I lie there, still, silent, catching, until it is my turn to ask, "What do you like?"

"I want you inside me." She removes the harness. She reaches under the bed again and pulls out a glove. She's on the bed now, face up. I put the glove on my right hand and begin to rub her clit slowly, softly. Sweat sweetly glistens on her body. I notice her triangle-style clitoral piercing—a silver ring, hanging—and I feel myself getting wet again. As my hand works her, I move my mouth to her neck. Biting. She likes it. Her moans tell me to bite harder. And I do. Her tits hang slightly to the sides of her body. Large, full, round. Nipples erect, waiting for my mouth.

Oh, yummy. The salty, sweaty taste of skin.

"More, put in more," she moans. "Yeah, fuck me harder. Yeah, like that."

I hope I'm not hurting her. Only two fingers left outside her swallowing cunt. Now just the thumb.

"Ooh, yeah, like that."

My whole fist is up there. And I fuck. I fuck like my hand could come, like if I fuck hard and deep enough, my hand will ejaculate. Faster. Her insides open up to me like a succulent lily. It's so warm in here. So squishy. So sexy.

Her breath quickens, and I can feel her lower back tighten. Harder. Faster. She lets it out. A moan saved up just for me. Her nails digging into my thighs. Her body goes limp. It's over.

I awaken the next morning and look around at my surroundings: Lipstick Boy jumping on velvet bedclothes.

Wow, it's still my birthday. She is more gorgeous than I remember.

Small talk. And it's time for me to go. I've got my legs hanging out the side van door. As I'm putting my boots on, I notice something all over the right thigh of my jeans. "What is that?" I wonder out loud.

She puts a hand down to her cunt and removes it, saying, "Oh, I guess that's me—I'm bleeding."

Oh, my God, bleeding! My only pair of pants for the weekend, and I've got some chick's menstrual blood all over them…and she lives in a van.

I collect myself, half laughing, half wanting to scream, as we say goodbye. I wish her well on her journeys. She wishes me a happy birthday. And just like it started, it ends. With a kiss. And her crimson stain on me. A birthday present for my memory.

And I go my way.

The Spanking Booth

RACHEL KRAMER BUSSEL

It's the one-year anniversary party for our local feminist dyke-run sex shop. I've been looking at the flier for this event since I first picked it up a few weeks ago, making up elaborate scenes of what it will be like. The flier promises go-go girls, party favors, and, most important (to me), a spanking booth. It sounds, especially to my sapphically inexperienced mind, like the coolest party around. By the time the actual date rolls around, my fantasies have become so elaborate that the real thing will probably pale in comparison. You see, even though I consider myself a gregarious, even boisterous person, I feel unsophisticated and nerdy around "real" dykes. They are "real" not because they are lesbian to my bi/pansexual nature, but "real" because they fully interact in the lesbian community, not just visiting it occasionally. "Real" because to my mind they (unlike me) aren't nervous about approaching women, about knowing what to do, and aren't overwhelmed with awe every time they make another girl come.

I'm anxious, excited, bursting with that kind of nervous energy that makes you want to get drunk, except I'm already drunk on my own giddiness. I've dressed in the most provocative thing I can find in my meager closet: short black skirt and see-through red mesh shirt (no bra), topped off with enough body glitter for a dozen people.

I go to a friend's apartment beforehand to watch a new porn video with some friends and kill time. We take a while to decide how we will get there and who's going or not going. Finally we head out the door. When we arrive, we have to wait in a long line, during which I sneak peeks at all the glittery, fabulously dressed girls also waiting to get in.

When we at last get to the front of the line, they almost don't let our group in because we have boys with us. But eventually they relent. I walk past the door guard and take in my surroundings: go-go dancers on stage, DJs spinning, a sexy photo exhibit, and all around me girls, girls, girls! I hang out with my friends for a while, nervously fidgeting with my clothes, wondering if I look totally ridiculous, half wanting to bolt out the door before someone calls my bluff.

I get to the bathroom and almost accept an invitation to join the girls in front of me in a stall, but then my secret shyness takes over. I avoid their eye contact and scurry into a stall by myself. When I emerge, I determinedly brave the crowds; I was promised a spanking booth, and damn it, I want to be spanked!

I enter another room and mingle, saying hello to the women from the shop, who are all decadently dressed up. I'm used to seeing them behind counters full of dildos and vibrators and lubes, but now they're here to party and celebrate, just like

Rachel Kramer Bussel

everyone else. And even though I don't really know them, I feel a kinship with them, a form of instant bonding when you know someone thinks like you and shares at least some of your interests. One of them, who has sold me some of my favorite sex toys, is dressed up all dominatrix-like. She tells me she does it professionally, and I'm quite impressed. I've admired this woman since I first saw her; she's always seemed confident, fun, and sexy. So seeing her in her dominatrix outfit only adds to her supercool aura.

I enter another room and spy two women I met a few nights ago. I try to figure out if they're together, but I'm left with mixed signals. I hang out again with my friends for a little while, still too nervous to head out on my own. Eventually, though, I decide that this was part of my reason for coming here, so I proceed upstairs without my friends, who are content to lounge at the bar downstairs.

I'm nervous but determined to go through with this. When I get upstairs I see some of the women who work at the store. They encourage me to go onstage, and they're really friendly, which sparks my confidence and makes me smile. I inch toward the stage and find the women I'd met the other night. They seem to be having a good time, taking in the go-go dancers and the exuberant dancing, jiggling crowd. I flirt with them by adorning their faces with some of my glitter, which I pull out of my bag. Then I ask them to hold my bag as I make my way forward. They gladly oblige. As I approach the stage, all of a sudden I realize a lot of people are watching, which makes me excited but also more nervous. Some of my determination and eagerness start to give way to a "well, maybe I shouldn't really do this" attitude. But as I wait my turn in line, I recall how much I've been looking forward to this and know that if I pass up the chance now, I'll be kicking myself forever.

When I get onstage, I feel like I'm in some special secret world, if only for a few minutes. I'm standing right near the spanker, the one I noticed earlier, whom I've admired surreptitiously in the past. I'm in awe that I'm only inches away from this incredibly beautiful woman who will soon spank me. And even though she's all done up in dominatrix garb, I feel like I could cuddle up against her. She exudes not just sex and domination, but an energy that fills with me pride and happiness, making me feel electrically charged before she even touches me. I want to wrap that sensation around me as protection. I feel like my face is bright red, and it probably is. I have the urge to giggle, but I suppress it.

Her assistant asks me which instrument I want to be spanked with, and for a(nother) moment, my bravado falters. I don't know what to pick! But instead of looking like a total fool by letting her use an instrument that would be too much for me, I shyly whisper my uncertainty, asking them which of the devices is the least painful. She picks a wooden paddle, and I bend over. I have on a filmy, light skirt, but even that is too much interference. I lift up my skirt and show off my leopard-print panties to the crowd. This is the moment I've been waiting for, and I don't want to miss a single stroke. As she spanks me, I marvel at the sensation—I've only had people use their bare hand on me; this is an altogether more extreme sensation. At first she gives me what feel like little taps that combine to create lots of heat and spark. Five of these tiny taps somehow feel like 20, and I'm thrilled to discover this technique.

I like the way she has to concentrate, working the paddle around my ass to give me the full experience. These are not just amateur whacks without any forethought but carefully designed thwacks to maximize impact. I could lose myself to this, go wild and wet and out of control, but I know this is only a short demonstration. When my time is up, I straighten my skirt, give my spanker a kiss on the cheek and hop off the stage, wishing there'd been time for more. My ass is red and only slightly sore, and I'm thrilled beyond belief. I've discovered that my delight in spanking is not just a moment's vanity or delusion but something real and true and gratifying. For me, the spanking was less a punishment than a reward. I know (or at least, hope) that spanking will now play a starring role in my sex life.

The friends I came with weren't there to witness my moment of glory, but that doesn't matter. I feel energized—a sort of natural high. I start talking to the women who held my bag. And, of course, it takes me a really long time to realize that one of them is flirting with me.

I feel so out of the loop, like I'll never "fit in" with the dyke scene, will never have an intuitive sense of when someone wants me. We keep talking and eventually go outside. She has to bluntly ask if she can come home with me before I fully get the point. Suddenly, I'm shy and nervous again. But I do take her home with me and celebrate another first.

And tonight I felt glamorous, decadent, slutty, sexy. Not bad for a novice.

Kim Like Bob

Lynne Herr

In South Korea the roads are dragster alleys, the bargoers play smoky macho games, the restaurants reek of fermented cabbage, and beautiful women are *everywhere*. Almost all are sexy and sleek by nature—even the shy girls, the young girls with their Hello Kitty hairpins and flared legs and perfect bangs. Waiting to marry so they can leave home.

Then there's the Korean dyke. The fringe element often sacrificing family and sometimes the entire family's honor to meet, smoke, and dance in quiet, dangerous spaces. At least that's how it was five years when I flew into Seoul as an English teacher. Five years ago, when I thought some of my friends were cute, assuming the feelings were isolated incidents…

Jana, a fellow teacher who always wore hats to cover her misguided foray into white-girl dreads, grabbed my hand late one night and tugged me from the American area downtown (drunk soldiers and burger joints) to "the only dyke bar in Korea." She knew I'd been to the Egyptian Room in Portland and had even kissed a few drunk girls, talking about how nice they smell, how much I dug drummers…but I didn't know if I was queer enough to be going to the *only dyke bar in Korea*.

"Shush. Do you speak Korean?"

"No. I can only read—"

"No need," she said, the purple threads in her skullcap picking up her nearly purple lipstick. "There're two female symbols out front on this tiny neon sign. I just want you to talk to this one girl for me. She speaks good English, but not enough to get my jokes. My Korean is fucking awful…"

She hailed a cab, gave the driver the cross streets, and sat back with me, talking about her crush. I watched our cabbie pinball through the crowded masses, nearly colliding with three drunk businessmen and a long BMW. The backseat smelled like soju and old shoes. Sticky brown pleather. Some things are universal.

"Her name's Ming and she's so hot. We danced last time. A waltz or some shit," Jana laughed.

The club sat between a "Coppee House" and a barbecue place where you cook your own meat on grills built into each tabletop, scoop it into lettuce leaves, add a hunk of garlic, some sprouts, red pepper paste, and blanched spinach, then eat. Lettuce, taco style.

"Hungry?" I asked, staring at my curly red hair reflected off the window, my ragged wool sweater and torn leather jacket. No makeup. Sneakers. Not exactly the kind of girl I thought would appeal to the standard impeccably dressed, fashion-conscious Korean lady.

"I'm not hungry. Stop stalling. I know you dig chicks. Let's go," she said, grabbing my hand again.

We walked down a small side alley to a brightly lit back door, where two drag kings greeted us. One eyed Jana up and down as we walked down the hallway to the bar. Jana looked over her shoulder playfully, her butt wiggling more than I'd ever seen. "It's still a little old-school with the butch/femme thing," she whispered.

"So what are you?" I asked, looking at her skirt *and* boots.

"Femme. Femmes get free drinks." She smiled back at the taller king.

At the end of the hallway, we reached a huge windowless room where about 15 women were scattered around, most of them smoking. Hip hop blared from crackling speakers high up on the paneled walls. A heavyset woman with a pompadour and black suit served drinks from behind the cherry-wood bar at the far end of the room, k.d. lang posters framed behind her.

"Hello," a gorgeous, bobbed boy-girl to my left called out. She stretched out her hand as if she were the owner.

"Hi. I'm Lynne. This is Jana," I said.

"I know Jana," she said, giving me a friendly look. "Come here." She winked, towing me to the bar for a mai tai, on her.

"That's OK. I got it," I awkwardly mumbled, offering some won.

"No, not *date*. Just friendly only," she smiled.

Jana had already struck up a conversation with some "Westernized" women along the back wall; one knew a friend of hers from New York. "Small world," Jana said—then explained what the saying meant. They laughed, holding their fingertips together in the shape of tiny world globes.

One of the women smiled at me with her head half bowed, but her eyes met mine. She wore a small plastic choker around her neck, black patent go-go boots under a sheer black skirt, and a baby tee. Rings on her thumbs. Fidgeting with the filter of her Marlboro Light.

I thanked my temporary host, then joined Jana.

"This is Kim and Sue. Kim and Sue, this is Lynne."

Korean schoolchildren take English names for class and often keep them when speaking to foreigners as adults. It's easier for foreigners to remember names familiar to them.

Sue also taught English, but in Pusan. Kim, the go-go boot chick, was off to college in Australia next week. She was drinking a red cocktail with yellow cherries and said her favorite movie star was Jodie Foster. "Of course," I laughed.

Kim and I sat down and started talking. She told me about the difficulties of being gay in Korea, how she decided to study international marketing as a way to leave her country but not her people, how she hoped someday to marry a gay man. Maybe even a gay Korean man. These things weighed heavily on her mind because she was, after all, nearly 28 years old.

"I'm too much a girl to live like a man," she told me—gesturing to the woman who'd bought me the mai tai. "She work with men and live like a man. But she left her village and her family."

Some funky Asian dance music blasted on, prompting all the ladies to hit the small dance floor in the far left corner. To me, most Korean dykes looked androgynous; I could only identify the "butch" chicks by whether they drank cocktails or beer, sat with their legs together or apart, laughed quietly or out loud. Kim drank cocktails, sat with her legs apart and laughed quietly. Two out of three. A versatile girl. What luck.

She held my hand while we danced. Swinging arms and smiling to the electronic drumbeats like a 1950s love story with the wrong soundtrack. Telling me she'd like to kiss me. She had only kissed two other women before, and they were both Australian.

"Oh—so that's why you're moving there."

"No," she giggled.

I leaned in and kissed her. The bartender clapped. When the song ended, she bought us both a shot of tequila. Said we looked sexy.

But sexy or not, it was time to close. The bartender yelled something to everyone as the lights came up.

32   Lynne Herr

"She is telling us to be careful. Last month a girl was hit when she left here. A very boyish girl. It can be bad."

"Where do you live?"

"Five kilometers away," she said, watching my mouth with her dark almond eyes.

"How do you get home?"

"I am staying tonight with Sue. Very close. We take a taxi."

"Oh…" I wondered if the underlying sense of duty and shame that pervaded most of South Korea's culture still held on to the foundations of even these fringe rebels. "Um…" I fumbled, not wanting to insult her, but knowing she would be gone in a week. I had to make my move.

"Where do you live?" she asked.

"About 15 minutes away by cab."

"By cab…oh, yes. Alone?" she asked, her face flushing as she reached for another cigarette from her black beaded handbag.

"I have a roommate, but she's in Japan this weekend."

"Ah…"

I lit her cigarette. The crowd moved out.

Jana tugged my arm. "My girlie Ming wasn't here. Oh, well. We headin' out?"

"Su-u-ure…"

Jana looked back and forth between us. "OK. How about I meet you out front? I'll be the only one outside alone." It's true, you hardly ever see anyone walking alone in Korea.

After Jana left and the 100-watt bulbs illuminated all the burns and scars on the dull wood floor, Kim kissed me again. A long, deep kiss. The kiss of someone ready to break open.

"Would you like to come home with me?" I finally asked.

"Yes," she whispered, this time keeping her eyes on the ground. Then she grabbed my hand, quickly kissed my knuckles and walked ahead of me up the back stairs into the damp fall air. My stomach flipped.

Jana was both pleased and disappointed that I was taking

Kim home. "I feel manic, and now I have to go home and talk to my cutouts." She had to leave her cat in the States, so she had taped photographs of him on her wall.

We grabbed a cab in no time. Kim translated my address and off we flew. She sat flat against her side of the cab, afraid to touch me. I wondered what she'd say when we starting having sex— what words in what language.

She leaned forward abruptly and told the driver to stop, then ran out without looking back. What the hell was that all about? I jumped out and ran after her after dropping too much cash on the front seat.

"Kim?" I called after her, bumping into people, stepping on discarded Coke cans.

I peeked in and around the crowd, following her with my eyes as she slowed to a brisk walk and turned down a small alley. I found her leaning against a dirty wall behind a dumpster. Bargoers poured out by the mouth of the alley, oblivious to us. We heard music cut off in the coffee shops and restaurants around us. Cabs honked.

"Kim?"

"I'm sorry. I can't. I want to, but I am afraid…if anything happens, then I would not go to Australia."

"I understand," I told her, standing with my hands in my pockets.

She pulled me into her. I put my arms around her waist, feeling the black beaded bag poking from the back of her skirt. We kissed slowly, timidly at first, each of us listening for footsteps or windows opening above.

Then the kissing intensified, and she drove her tongue into my mouth. I gingerly moved my hands down to the hem of her skirt.

"Don't go slow. I want this," she instructed, her eyes shining.

"OK." And I took control, acting like I'd done this a million times. I moved my hand slowly under her skirt, wiggling inside her tights, pulling them down a bit in the front. She gasped.

Her hands moved quickly up the front of my sweater, rubbing my hard nipples through the wool. She sucked on my neck.

"Touch me," she whispered.

I felt her wetness through her underwear as I rubbed her clit up and back. Kim grabbed my shoulder with one arm and ran her hand up my sweater with the other. She groaned quietly. I could feel she was hard enough to come, so I stopped.

I kissed her again, this time moving her hand to undo my zipper. She shoved her hand deep inside my jeans, imitating what I'd done to her. I started jerking her off again with the same beat.

Her hand stopped; she was too distracted by her own feelings to concentrate on me. I reached down and picked up where she'd left off, rubbing her with my right hand and myself with my left. She watched me intently, leaned back against the wall, and spread her legs farther apart.

Touching her while I touched myself felt almost like I was watching myself in a mirror, feeling exactly the way she felt. I imagined coming into her. She mumbled something in Korean, grabbed my nipples hard, and pulled me close to her. I stopped, thinking I'd heard someone at the mouth of the alley.

"Go…" she said.

She braced herself against the wall, sucking in shallow, fast breaths with closed eyes. I leaned my forehead against the wall, feeling urgent and hot and dizzy.

I moved my fingers from myself and put them in her mouth. She lapped up the taste of me while I circled her swollen clit until she came, teeth against my fingers. Then I took a step back and jerked myself off with her leaning against the wall, lighting a cigarette, telling me she likes to watch me….

We smoked together on the slowly emptying street corner, waiting for separate cabs. She told me she had a wonderful time: "It was crazy!"

A cab pulled over for me and I hopped in. I told her I'd write a story about the experience someday. Kim asked me to change her name, then she laughed. "Oh, I am like Bob in the United States!"

"You're not like any Bob I've ever known," I said out the window as my speed-racer dragster screeched away.

Drag Kings

Flaunting It

ELISE CHAPMAN

My Daddy and I always had trouble fitting into the "real world." No one understood the depth and strength of our relationship. To friends, we were fun-loving eccentrics. To most others, we were self-centered women determined to antagonize the proverbial moral majority. I'd heard it a thousand times before—Texas drawls full of conditional tolerance: "I don't care what they do behind closed doors so long as they don't flaunt it." Or insulting compliments from well-meaning relatives: "Can't you please go out with a man again? You are too pretty to waste." And let's not forget the ever-popular suggestion: "If you really want to be with a woman, you should find one that looks like a woman." Even some lesbians were put off by our antics: "You mean you call your girlfriend 'Daddy'? That's sick!"

Confusion? Perversion? Flaunting? I didn't understand. What could be more conventional than a dad taking his boy out for some wholesome father-son bonding?

Our time had come. After months of private games behind closed doors, Daddy had finally decided to dress me up and show me off in public. A queer rite of passage, if you will.

Dressing for Success

We were eager to step out on the town, but not before a shopping spree at the local thrift store for discount men's apparel. The world of menswear was foreign to me. I'm a femme whose fag-boy alter ego had never manifested itself physically. Dressing up certainly proved to be physically challenging for me. The two athletic bras were simply not enough to flatten my D-cup breasts, but I didn't fret much over my disguise. No matter how tightly I bound my chest, my ass would always be a dead giveaway. Although I knew I couldn't pass as a man, the thought of adventure spurred me on.

While Daddy dressed calmly in the living room, I struggled with the rest of my gear in the privacy of my bedroom: tighty whiteys, khakis, a preppy white button-down, an ageless polyester navy sports jacket, and the absolute gem of the thrift search, a classic 1980s new wave leather necktie. Black leather to boot. Every bad boy's favorite.

"Daddy, can you help me?" I walked out, fumbling with my tie, only to come face-to-face with my ruggedly handsome lover in full Daddy regalia. It was basically the same outfit as mine, but with decidedly more attention to detail. Her tie was neatly knotted, her secondhand shirt was pressed, and her pants boasted a proper manly bulge.

"Come here, boy. On your knees." I obeyed without argument. She inspected the shoulder seams on my jacket and ran one hand through my long blond hair. "Looks good, but first we're gonna to have to do something about this mess," she said in her Texas-tinged voice as she clutched a wad of hair at the nape of my neck. "I don't want no hippie boy." In a sudden gesture of affection, she rammed my cheek into her lumpy crotch. My signal to obey. I slicked my feminine mane into a discreet ponytail.

"OK, much better," she said. "Now for the tie." She folded the narrow band, popped it like a belt, then looped it around my neck in a menacing fashion. Not quite sure whether she would tie it or choke me with it, I closed my eyes to escape, but I couldn't avoid the smell of cigarettes on her breath and the aftershave she had splattered onto her sadly hairless face. She grabbed the collar of my shirt and twisted lightly. "Hey! Open your eyes, sissy boy. What's wrong? Scared of your old man?" She laughed, then kissed me with an intensity that caused a moistness in my cotton briefs. I wondered how it was possible for a boy to get so wet from a necktie.

The inspection continued. Her hand slid down my shirt, pausing to interpret the tautness of my double bra and compressed breasts. She thumped my chest. "Good job. Nice strong pecs. You're growing up, gettin' to be a big boy." Her touch moved farther down my torso, ultimately stopping at the obvious bagginess in my crotch. I was missing an essential element: the dick.

Although Daddy had identified as butch all her life, she had minimal experience with packing her pants. After some consideration, she bypassed all the more pliable rubber options for an unharnessed yet functional silicone model affectionately nicknamed "Blue Boy." Daddy ordered that I don a small but tough silicone dick. Tough was right. The base wedged itself into my lips and the stiff shaft pressed up into my abdomen. Luckily the briefs were tight enough to hold it steady, though it was a bit uncomfortable. *Grin and bear it,* I told myself as I admired my bulky new package in the mirror. *Take it like a man.*

Leather Family

With cocks and ties in place, we were ready for a night of gender-bending escapades. We set out on her souped-up motorcycle, a father and son in mismatched suits on their way to a pansexual leather dinner.

When I made my debut in the dining room, all eyes pounced on me. No one had ever seen me in drag, and the shock on their faces disturbed my fragile composure. Suddenly I joined the world of awkward 12-year-old boys. Horny but scared. Restless. Shifting back and forth on my feet in hopes of figuring out how to stand like a man. The truth was that as a man I was hopelessly effeminate and doomed to finish out my life as a queer little fag boy. The idea was strangely appealing.

Before long, I had an entourage of inquiring minds breathing down my neck. There were hetero dommes, bisexual wives, swinging husbands, butch boys, gay men, and even bi-curious male submissives. I felt studly, as if everybody wanted a piece of my action. Male privilege was mine at last. Even the dyke daddies who had ignored me as a daddy's girl loved me as a daddy's boy.

Daddy's good buddy Sir Francis approached me with a flame in her eye that burned from my neck to my pants. I became suddenly aware of the vulnerability of my crotch. The dildo stuck out like a sore thumb, so to speak. The rigid corners of the base dug into the upper folds of my labia, threatening my clit. When proper pressure was applied it made me hard, but one incorrect move and I would crumble like a real man.

"What did you do to her?" Sir Francis asked my daddy jokingly. "Where did the beautiful femme go?" Beautiful femme? I hadn't thought she had ever noticed me.

"I'm a boy tonight," I announced eagerly. "I bet you didn't

know that about me." Smiling, she turned to my daddy for affirmation.

"Yeah, this is my boy, Tony. He's one fine young 'un, isn't he?"

"He sure is." Sir Francis whispered something in Daddy's ear, and before I knew it, her presence was towering over me. She looked me in the eye and without warning placed her strong, skillful hand over the dildo hidden in my pants. Sir Francis was more than aware of what she was doing; she seemed determined and even slightly sadistic. I gasped. My clit was being assaulted, and I couldn't decide if it was for better or for worse. I looked to Daddy for help.

"It's OK, boy. I won't let Sir Francis hurt you too bad."

I wasn't so sure.

After one final stroke to my cock and clit, I let out a girlish squeal that turned heads in the rest of the restaurant. Daddy grabbed my elbows from behind and kissed my ear.

"Now tell Sir Francis thank you, boy."

I bowed my head and squeaked. "Thank you, sir."

My assailant just chuckled and walked away. Even though Sir Francis was a dyke, she sure knew her way around a boy's pants.

Atomic Café

Next stop was Atomic Café, an underground all-ages bar, for "Fetish Night." The fact that the clientele was primarily hetero didn't faze us. The title alone sounded promising. *Fetish. Fetish. Fetish.* It echoed in my little boy head like a forgotten fairy tale. I envisioned a utopia where I would be free to express my various sordid fantasies in public. Daddy and I would pay our $2 cover to enter a world that approximated a perverted family reunion. Or so it was in our dreams.

We walked through the black curtain only to find a bar full of underage goth kids smoking cloves. Not exactly our scene, but the theatrical spanking demonstration on the stage engaged us instantly. Although we didn't blend in, no one paid us much notice.

After several beers, we embarked upon the dreaded journey to the restroom.

"Daddy, can I ask you something?"

"Yes, boy. What is it?"

"Which bathroom?" It was a valid question. We opted for the women's room since we didn't want to deal with the stress of urinals and male bonding.

Daddy took the first available stall. Shortly after she went in, I heard a thump and then a scream from her neighbor. Daddy's distinct Houston accent followed the commotion.

"Damn! I lost my dick!"

I bent down and looked under the door just in time to witness a petite foot in the adjoining stall nervously kick Blue Boy. Daddy's big blue dildo rolled back into the proper stall but not before collecting several shreds of toilet paper on its sticky surface.

"Sorry," Daddy said to her neighbor through the wall. "This damn dick. Just can't keep it in my pants sometimes! Hee, hee, hee."

I wasn't amused. I was the one left squirming outside with six young vampiras shying away from me as if I were a monstrous garlic clove.

Things took a turn for the worse when Daddy emerged with her pants halfway unzipped and the blue dick in her hand. "I can't put this baby back in my shorts without washing it." By that time all eyes were peeled. "Nope. Sure can't. You know why, little boy?" She caught me by the arm during my attempt to flee into the empty stall and whispered in my ear, "Because you're gonna give Daddy some extra special attention once we get out of here."

When I came back out, she was still at work cleaning the dildo, and I joined her at the sink. Most of the bewildered girls had scattered at that point, but two brave ones lingered, smoking and gossiping by the paper towel dispenser. To distract myself, I reached for my lipstick and powder only to find that I had no purse. I forgot—boys don't wear makeup and carry bags, or at least not in that bar. Maybe a gay bar with drag queens would be more our style. We decided to leave.

Chain Drive

Daddy led me across the main roads of the queer district on my dog leash. Unfortunately the street was no longer so queer-friendly due to some trendy mainstream bars recently erected in the area. The roaring SUVs at the red light emitted a slew of drunken threats and insults.

"Fuckin' fags!"

"Freaks!"

"Hey, it's dykes!" Bee-e-eep! "Can I watch? Ha! Ha!"

I fixed my eyes on Daddy's strong hand holding my leash. "What's wrong with these people?" I asked. "Can't they see we're on a date?" Some boys are so rude. Their daddies must not have raised them right.

I took consolation in the fact that we wouldn't see those loudmouths at the Chain Drive. It was one of the seediest locales in town and the only true leather bar. Daddy and I paraded in our suits through the main room, straight past the pool tables, the pinball machines, the bear flags, and the interesting mixture of gay men. There were no drag queens. We were the closest thing to women in the entire bar.

On the shadowy back patio, no societal rules apply. One solitary he-man in the corner was rubbing his package absent-mindedly. The signal was soon picked up by a muscular couple in leather harnesses who approached him for a group jack-off session.

Most of the men wore Levi's and macho tank tops. However, I spotted one particularly strange character, a stocky fellow in a ripped-up *Flashdance* T-shirt, chains, and demonic face paint who talked incessantly to anyone who came within 10 feet of his table. He was the only one making noise other than the groans and mumblings that came from the patio's periphery. He ranted on and on to an unfortunate bystander. "And then I told him, 'No, I won't fuck you. You're fat and ugly.' And do you know what that small-dicked son of a bitch did? He threw a drink in my face. Of all the nerve."

The disgruntled demon boy was trying to interrupt anyone having more fun than he was, which was practically the entire bar. Nearby I saw one young preppy couple screwing in the corner and a master in black leather pants getting a blow job from his slave.

Daddy took a seat on a park bench in the darkest corner possible. I followed the orange ember of her cigarette and sat on her knee.

"This is more like it," she said as she guided my hand to her fly. Instinctively I unzipped her pants. What next? It had been years since I had done anything that even remotely resembled cock sucking, except for the occasional lollipop. Since I was exclusively with women, I never expected to suck another dick again in my life. But life is full of surprises, right?

"Boy, seein' as you've turned out so faggy with your prissy strut and long hair, I figure I need to break you in the right way." She reached over and gave my dildo a couple of good, hard strokes. "Do you know what fag boys do for their daddies?"

"No." My loud gulp inspired her to squeeze my cock even more adamantly. The friction enlarged my clit considerably, and I began to understand how it felt to be jacked off.

"Pull a chair over here and sit in front of me. I'll teach you how." I returned with the chair to find Daddy smiling with her legs slightly spread and her fist stabilizing the blue dildo through her zipper.

"Come here. Give Daddy a kiss."

"OK." I leaned over and kissed her on the mouth.

"No, not there, silly. Here." She motioned downward to the menacing piece of silicone. I took the lifeless dark blue head into my lips and looked up at her. As soon as my mouth made contact, she felt it. I knew it was real, as did the group of spectators we had attracted. Her cock had come to life inside my mouth, throbbing and searching inside the hot wetness for the key to all fantasies. I suddenly had the power to make anything possible for my Daddy…and for myself.

"Deeper, boy. Show these men how good you can make Daddy feel." I gasped, my eyes watering from the jabs into my soft palate. "Take it!" Once again I gagged and swallowed. "That's a good boy," she said as she stroked my hair, which at that point was coming loose from my ponytail. "Good boy. You're learning now. I want to see you get your face fucked. I want to hear you take it all. Go on. Take it." She pressed my head down so that my throat had no choice but to engulf the entire length of silicone. There was no escape.

"Get ready. Daddy's gonna come in your mouth. Be a good boy and take all Daddy's come." I wouldn't dare stop. "Here it is, boy. Here it is. Get ready!" With that, Daddy thrust Blue Boy deep into my skull. I kept still until her spasms were over. My lover then tugged lightly on my chain in a motion for me to sit back up. We were both spent.

Daddy leaned back in the chair, still smoking a cigarette. Sometimes she looked at me, her faithful boy, and other times she glanced around proudly toward the curious male onlookers. *Who are these people?* the leathermen must have wondered. *And what are they? Fags? Chicks with dicks?* We definitely didn't look like the typical Chain Drive clientele. After all, no self-respecting regular would wear a suit and tie to a leather bar.

Coming Home

Home at last. My girlfriend dropped me off and headed out on her bike. After a night of flaunting my most taboo perversion in public, I was ready for some privacy. First, I stripped down and set my suffocating breasts free. With the removal of each article of clothing, the boy in the mirror faded more and more into the distance. It was strange to see a curvaceous woman emerge in men's underwear sporting a stiff, diagonal bulge in front. I ran my hand across my concealed weapon and pondered the fate of my little black dildo that had yet to make a public appearance. Instead of setting the toy aside with my other accoutrements, I pulled the dampened crotch of my briefs over and guided my toy into the dark pink haven that Daddy's dick had begged to visit all night.

Before long, my right hand grazed the white cotton over my small female mound. When the shy caresses turned ferocious, I knew I had to have more. I dug through the flaps of the fly so that one hand could rub my clit while the other thrust the dildo deep inside my cunt. I couldn't hold back anymore.

In a panting frenzy, I speed-dialed the phone. "Daddy, may I come now?"

"Yes, you may." I heard a voice behind me say. Just in time. Daddy hadn't left after all. Of course not. Voyeurs and exhibitionists are inseparable. Through our lengthy search around town, we had finally found our niche in each other.

Daddy sauntered over to my quivering, sweaty body sprawled out on the bed. The night had just begun.

Lady Luck

MISS FORTUNE

I must be the only chick on earth who goes to Vegas to unwind. Hey, some folks like to meditate in the Sierra Nevadas—all I need to feel content and Zenlike is a budget-priced room somewhere near Las Vegas Boulevard. As a retreat from the Lexus SUVs, smog, and transsexual whores of my adopted City of Angels, I eke out solace in the casino trams, Benson & Hedges stench, and $2.99 steak buffets of Sin City.

My fascination with Vegas began when I was a little girl—when my grandpa taught me how to play poker, and instead of using chips to bet, we used Coffee Nips and Werther's Originals from Grandma's crystal candy dish. I was an expert gambler by age 11. Little did Grandpa know I could read the reflection of his hand in his horn-rimmed glasses.

I was further intrigued when I saw the movie *Bugsy*, that Warren Beatty flick about the Jewish mafia, about how Ben "Bugsy" Siegel created this entertainment oasis in the middle of the desert with hard-won mob money. That film finally made it cool to be a Jew—as though having some shady criminal background in one's genes makes one automatically hip in that Scorsese kinda way. But hey, I'd rather be stereotyped as calculating and intimidating than as some neurotic, nebbishy Woody Allen type.

But what really sparked my interest in the seedy glitz of Las Vegas was when I caught *Viva Las Vegas* on TBS during some Elvis Marathon about five years ago. Hell, yeah, Ann-Margret was indeed a stunning siren in her formfitting black capris, but it was Elvis Presley as Lucky Jackson who really inspired me. God, the charisma that man had! A curl of the lip, a tilt of the pelvis, and every Bettie Page look-alike within a 100-mile radius was swooning with desire. If only I had that effect on women...

Of course, I've tried. To think of the countless hours I've spent dyeing my hair Nice 'n Easy blue-black, buzzing it, painstakingly distributing Royal Crown pomade from the mousy brown roots to the Wonder Woman–black tips. And the wages I've squandered on dark-rinse denim, wallet chains, and wing-tip creepers—all for naught once I realized that no matter what the hell I'm wearing, I'm just too friggin' femme-looking to pull off that rugged greaser look—it must be my goddamn big tits and dainty hands.

So I've come to terms with the fact that I'm one of those "femme in the streets, butch in the sheets" kinda dykes. And though I might be wearing a tight black sweater, a skintight leopard miniskirt, fishnets, and Cuban heels, I can still fix an engine on a '50 Ford better and faster than any of the macho, pompadoured, car-club poseur guys who have shown up here at the Gold Coast Hotel and Casino for this year's Viva Las Vegas Rockabilly Weekender.

✠ ✠ ✠

Jenna is here with me this year. Haven't seen her in about two years, since I moved from Atlanta to L.A. Our relationship has been long and rocky, but I just love the woman; I mean, we have a history. We've been friends and on-and-off lovers since we were both 16-year-olds wrapped up in our punk-rock angst, spending our lofty part-time cashier's salaries on X albums, Wet 'n' Wild nail polish, and nasty skunk weed we'd score from our skinny, pasty goth boyfriends.

I remember the first time we got together. It was 13 years ago. Jenna's boyfriend at the time, Jason, a pimply Nick Cave wanna-be with really bad B.O., was the only guy we knew with a car, a loden-green VW bus. He'd used his fake ID to get us some Bushmills at Toco Hills Giant Package. We parked behind an abandoned roller rink off 78 and sucked the burning whiskey down with Dr Pepper chasers. Jenna and I were hiccuping and dancing like Rockettes in the shaky gravel parking lot as Jason looked on from his driver's seat, tapping his thumb against the steering column to the beat of "Nazi Punks Fuck Off," which was emanating from his cheap car stereo speakers. I was wearing my tight Siouxsie T-shirt and a black velvet skirt, my hair a chaotic Aqua Net halo of porcupine quills, and Jenna had donned a flame-colored turtleneck, which barely cloaked her pointy, corklike nipples, erect in the damp night air.

"Hey, are y'all gonna get all sick and shit and pass out on me tonight? Fuckin' lightweights!" Jason whined from the van. He fired up some pot and walked over to Jenna and me. "Here," he proffered, "why don't you take the first hit, Lori?" He handed me the thickly rolled joint, and I inhaled deep and slow, self-conscious about the rise and fall of my teenage 36Ds as I let the smoke fill my lungs.

Next thing I remember was playing Truth or Dare and Jason daring us to take off our tops. Then the flash of cold against my voluminous breasts…then, inexperienced male fingers, winding my nipples like an alarm clock. And suddenly I glanced downward, blushing, anxious, my cunt pulsating in anticipation when another hand met my breasts, a polished index finger softly tickling the sensitive topography of my large, tumescent nipples. Jenna's creamy white hand…the long fingers and chewed-up nails lacquered in glittery purple paint. The gentle hand that became fierce with each digit she slipped into the burning, soaked folds of my pussy.

It was Jenna who helped me realize I'm a lesbian. And Jenna who continued to flirt and then sleep with every goddamn bohemian guy she met at the all-ages club we frequented. Jenna who would cry on my shoulder when the inevitable breakups happened and she felt fucked over. Jenna who got trashed and told me her darkest secrets in her Georgia drawl and wept on my bathroom floor after she told me about the abortion she'd had. And Jenna who moved in with me for two years, sharing bath towels and pillows and stoned Sunday afternoons kissing on the couch…until she slept with Phil, Phil with his fucking Web company and loft downtown. And I took my tax return, my dog, and my beat-up Plymouth Valiant to Los Angeles to start my life anew (instead of having sweet dreams about you).

But I'm not into burning bridges, even the ones that lie over troubled water. And Jenna will always be my first love. There's no substitute for that history—no matter how checkered and dysfunctional—with anyone. I can forgive. So we've been keeping tabs on each other. Phil moved to San Jose last May. And Jenna looks ravishing tonight, smoking nonchalantly, slipping quarters into the Betty Boop slot machine, her narrow, tight ass enveloped in vintage crepe—my own Audrey Hepburn. Classy trailer trash in Vegas. Pink Ladies. Laverne and Shirley with bullet bras. Bad girls like back in high school, but we're both inching reluctantly toward 30.

✠ ✠ ✠

Over our Manhattans at the bar by the $10 pai gow tables, Jenna keeps mentioning this guy she's been E-mailing from Chicago—she thinks he'll show up for the weekender 'cause she saw him at the one in Indy I missed last year. She says he's really into hot rods and loves Johnny Cash. I try to act coolly interested and totally impartial, but I know how I feel is completely transparent once my eyes look heavenward in dismissal. When she senses my discomfort, she just chuckles huskily, looks at me all devil-eyed, and says that he's been hitting on her online but she's just not interested.

Shit, I love poker and blackjack, but I'm really not into these other games. I decide to ignore her fence-sitter shenanigans and focus on tonight's band lineup: western swing from Hot Club of Cowtown; old-school doo-wop from the Treniers; the croony singer of "Poon-Tang," Deke Dickerson; and a living legend, the original riot grrrl, Wanda Jackson, a growling kitten who wore clingy cashmere and fucked Elvis back in the day. Yeah! That's what I'm here for: Wanda Jackson. Wanda Jackson and the car show they're having tomorrow morning at the top level of the parking garage. Black patent Studebakers with flaming hoods. Turquoise '57 Chevys with whitewalls. I am not here—I mean it, damn it—to overanalyze my flighty best friend and lover(?).

✠ ✠ ✠

By the time we make it upstairs to the dance hall, I'm too busy trying to keep my balance to worry about Jenna. And a moment of drunken lucidity tells me to curb my tendency to obsess about the woman I'm with. Hey, I hardly ever get to see Jenna, and I should appreciate the time I have with her.

Deke Dickerson is onstage in a gold Manuel western shirt. Across the rickety wooden dance floor, there are voluptuous bombshells with swallows and cherries tattooed on their cleavage. The boys pose, greased hair a little too clean to be edgy, wearing bleached wife beaters, the requisite spiderweb tats on the elbows. Nobody with half the charisma of the King…

Jenna asks me to hold her Lucite purse when one of these slick boys asks her to dance. I oblige, but the whole time I'm watching her circle skirt balloon in time to the upright bass, I can feel the heat rise from my neck to my scalp. There's got to be a fucking brick in her purse, and damn it, I'm trying to carry it *and* my souvenir boot mug, now half full of lukewarm screwdriver. And sue me, I don't fucking dance.

But Jenna's floating on air. Blondie with his new 501s is picking her up and playing with her like she's some doll, grabbing her ass, twirling her lithe little body, and she's enjoying every second of it, seeming to forget that I'm here—her best friend since high school. The first woman she ever… *God, Lori. She's straight, fer chrissake! Always has been. Just made an exception for us to be together.* And so she'd have someone to hold her motherfucking 10-ton retro purse while she swings to Deke doin' "Lady Killin' Papa." She always loved lying back and letting me do all the work.

I refill my souvenir mug with straight Bushmills, drop her purse at the edge of the dance floor, and angrily stomp out of the dance hall. I don't need this shit. The smug expression she wore, knowing she was ruling the dance floor. It brought me back to those Friday nights at Club Visage, me snorting rush in the bathroom while she made the social scene, teasing every 17-year-old Mohawked guy with a quick brush against their knee. Overcompensating…trying to cover up what we shared.

I shuffle past the Pall Mall–smoking housewives in their Bead-Dazzler sweatshirts, their eyes glazed over as they press the lit buttons of the video poker machine. Japanese tourists with disposable cameras take pictures of the bathroom doors.

I make my way outside. Cold desert air. An odd, soothing quiet. Neon in the distance flashing dates for David Cassidy and Sheena Easton at the Rio and a $4.99 surf-and-turf deal voted Best in Las Vegas. I brush away a stray tear and go to my favorite place, my safe haven: the parking garage.

The cold concrete and humming fluorescent lights here are somehow comforting to me. There's nobody here except for the tawny-colored, middle-aged security guard, snoozing on his putty folding chair on P1, a tattered copy of the *Las Vegas Sun* shrouding his ample lap. I stumble tipsily up the stairs to the rooftop level, the smell of urine, diesel, and Simple Green wafting in the stairwell.

All the classic cars and customs are parked here already for tomorrow's show. What a feast for my gearhead eyes: a Munster hearse with Rat Fink airbrushed on the hood. A '58 Bel-Air with chrome so shiny I can see my reflection in the bumper. I lose myself in admiration.

"Hey, there," a hoarse voice calls out. I thought I was alone.

"This one's a beaut, ain't it?" he says, his figure coming from behind the hood of a candy apple–red '62 Rambler. He's maybe 5 foot 8, kinda wiry, flames tattooed on his muscled arms, jet-black hair.

"Oh, uh, yeah," I say feebly.

"This one's mine. Been working on it for about nine months now—so it really is my baby in a way," he laughs. I notice his azure eyes, the eyelashes for days. The crooked sneer. Jeez, he's got a face like Elvis during his military years.

"Well, you've done some beautiful work here," I tell him.

"Thank you. Thank you very much. And what're you doing out here instead of inside where all the action is?" He smells like Irish Spring mixed with Castrol.

"Well, I think I just got dumped." I swig the Bushmills from my plastic boot.

"Yeah, I know the feeling. My girlfriend's up there dancing with some guy I don't even know. I think he's a fuckin' Brit."

"And I don't even dance," we say in unison, and the whiskey tingles like astringent on my brain. I let out a belly laugh.

"Can I have this dance, darlin'?" He grabs me, and we do a clumsy two-step to some imaginary steel guitar. Spinning in the brisk air. Whoo! Dizzy, and…I feel it then, that strangely familiar stiffness pressed hard against my soft backside. Man! I haven't felt that in so long. I allow my ego to be stroked; I've still got it, even if Jenna doesn't want it. He's rock-solid under his jeans and…

His lips are so soft. Pink and tender like a good steak. Tastes like Michelob and Camels. I can't help myself. He licks my mouth, his snaky tongue outlining my upper lips; licks down my neck until it's tracing my collarbone. His dexterous hands unbutton my cardigan. My blood boils, and it feels like my heart is pounding in my clit, in my silk panties, drenched with want. For a…*man.*

He grunts as he cups my ass cheeks with his sturdy hands, then shoves me down on the cold hood of the Rambler…his fingers are smooth and pale, and there's a millimeter of grime under his chopped nails. The fingers grasp at my underwear, tugging fast and gracelessly, slipping inside me until I feel their calluses and bone and soft skin, one by one. And then I gasp as the knuckles of a strong fist ram themselves into my constricted wet pussy, fast, forceful, male, hard. For the first time in 13 years, I want a cock.

Now.

But I'm being tortured. I have to wait here, hungry to be filled. He takes his fist out of my cunt and pushes his juicy fingers into my mouth. I taste my own come, the sweet and musky sweat from my bush hair, and his greasy fingers under all the dampness.

I reach for the straining bulge in his pants, that Tom of Finland–style thick rod that's protruding from his worn jeans. I'm gonna take every last bit of those eight inches and suck him absolutely dry. Goddamn it, I'm a butch fucking dyke, but I *know* how to use my friggin' mouth.

I undo the button fly, feeling a rush of power. He's gonna be putty in my hands now. Men'll do anything if you suck their dick—I remember that from high school.

Boxers, the trail of dark hair, the…the eight inches…of…a black leather dildo.

Under the bowling shirt, tiny tits, the subtle outline of a feminine rib cage.

Mm-m-m.

The King is alive.

And I should've known.

The King is alive, pumping furiously in my milky hole.

The leather burns good. It scrapes against my convulsing walls, branding me with its friction as I flail and gasp for air. As much as I wanna be the butch in charge, I just…can't…resist…dear fucking God…I surrender to this full-throttle fuck.

When I reach for her tits, she grabs my wrists and firmly cuffs them with her fingers. Nope. Tonight she's the boss. She's in, out, in, out, in, out—fast and powerful like a V8 engine— fucking crucifying my scorching slit, my ass making heart-shaped dents on the cold, hard hood of the car.

The grease from her hair is dripping onto my flushed breasts. Her firm, marbly nipples glide across my stomach, and my areolae rise to meet them. She abruptly lets me up, pushing my face down and shoving the drenched leather cock into my parched, anxious mouth.

"C'mon, girl, get my dick wet! You can do it now. Time for a little goddamn 'Jailhouse Cock'." Her eyes are little baby-blue slits when I look up. She's pushing her leather rod so fast into my mouth I nearly choke.

"Good girl," she says breathily. "Oh, yeah. You are one good little girl."

She manhandles me, picks me up with a brute force and throws me into the back seat. I hit my head on the back window, dizzy but oblivious to any pain. And suddenly I'm face-down on the faux leopard slipcover. She pulls me up by the waist, rams her prick into my tight virgin asshole, a harsh yet sweet pain ripping at my very core—that core I never let anyone touch. Her palm writhes manically over my bulbous, crimson clit.

And I come. And come again. Enough to fill a shot glass. She immediately puts her pillowy lips between my fleshy thighs and drinks me straight, no Dr Pepper chaser. She slurps from me as though she hasn't had water for a month, as though my snatch were an oasis.

I hear the faint strains of Wanda Jackson singing "Riot in Cell Block #9."

I look up to the star-riddled desert sky, a blinking reflection of a neon sign on the moon that reads: LONG LIVE THE KING.

✠ ✠ ✠

When I awaken two hours later, I smell her sex—my sex, *our* sex—but she's not in the car. I guess Elvis has left the building…

I dress halfheartedly and meander back to the dance hall.

"Lori! Where have you been?" Jenna asks me. "Man, I've been looking for you! I wanted to introduce you to Mike, you know, my friend from Chicago!"

It's her. She flashes me a knowing wink, extending her skilled hand to mine for a polite shake.

And I'm not gonna call her on her bluff. I just shake her hand and grin back.

Viva Las Vegas!

Chix in Bars, Chix at Parties

Last Tango in Paris, Texas

BETH GREENWOOD

You know the El Rio? Down on Cortez? Well, I'm not surprised; I'd be surprised if you did. It's not exactly what you'd call a memorable "establishment." Nothing, really, but a cinder block bunker in the middle of a red-dust parking lot. Hell, you wouldn't even know it was a bar except for the pieces of neon in the black, narrow strip of window. It didn't even say "El Rio" anymore—so maybe you know the E_ _io? Down on Cortez?

Whatever. It was the dive of dives, the black hole of Paris, Tex., frequented, as far as I know, by alcoholic kangaroo rats and inebriated rattlers, or at least the two-legged equivalents.

I do know that once a year for two or three days, during the gay pride observance, the owner hung a very tired rainbow flag in the doorway. I liked that a lot. I mean, as far as I know he wasn't a fag (and don't tell me a gal ran the place), but for a couple of days a year he looked up from the red dust, the flickering Budweiser sign, and looked us right in the eyes.

It wasn't really "our" place. We didn't have that kind of relationship; we just hadn't picked up those kinds of things—no song, no holiday, no place. It was just Shelly and me, the thin blond and the big butch. Just in case you haven't figured it out yet, I'm the butch and she's the blond. We didn't have a certain place, but we'd been to the El Rio before, and that little queer oasis just seemed to me to be the right kind of place to end it.

It wasn't like I didn't care for her. God knows we'd been up and down the ride enough times together. It was just…well, it was just over. I had this girlfriend back in the '70s who used to get real stoned and then real perceptive. One of my favorite insights of hers is that dykes just have so much juice in them, like gasoline. They run hot and fast and then, well, there's just nothing left. We just run out of gas. Rattle, rattle, gasp, sputter…nothin'. Who wants to push a relationship along? Not me, that's for sure.

I think Shelly knew this was it. I'm not great at hiding my feelings; good enough, though, because that one girl back in the '70s didn't see the breakup coming. Not before she looked me straight in the eyes and said, "Beth, you always make the wrong decisions."

Fuck you, bitch. I've made my share, but I've also scored a few times. My truck started out just a rusty pile of shit, but it became a thing of beauty after I got through with it. I've got a pretty good job. Working in a print shop isn't exactly brain surgery, but I've done a lot worse.

With Shelly and me…it was just over. Didn't need to see a lot more to know it just wasn't working. It had been fun, but the gauge was tapping E and the engine was seriously sputtering.

That morning we'd rolled out of bed like every other and

crawled into our stuff. The usual denim work shirt and jeans for me, with boots of course; pink turtleneck and cotton dress for her. We didn't say a lot, but that wasn't anything new. We'd been slipping down that quiet road for months. Still, it wasn't like we hated each other. Just ran out of gas.

I still loved her, but I'd taken the capital letter off that months ago. She still made me laugh, and I still looked at her with that fluttering thing in my stomach, but just not as much. I knew I'd miss seeing her when I came home from work, sitting there at the kitchen table reading Carlos Castaneda, Aleister Crowley, Margot Adler, or some such shit, something classical booming on the stereo (we'd gotten four complaints the first month she'd been living with me). Clove cigarettes. Haunting the flea markets for weird stuff. Little trips across the border. Sudden volleyball games with crunched-up typewriter paper. The poster for *The Burning Times,* which was one of her favorite things. At first we talked a lot, but then we started being just roommates and, recently, almost strangers.

I'd driven by the El Rio the night before, seen the rainbow flag, and suggested we go out for beers. I had my whole speech prepared, a little combo of what had worked for me before, spiced with a few words I thought she might like: "destined," "allowing us to follow our paths," and so forth.

It was night by the time we showered and shaved (or at least she shaved), the bright sodium lights making the city look like one of those weird pieces of jewelry she picked up. I smiled at that as I drove the truck down Cortez.

The place was deserted. Dirty linoleum floor, red plastic stools, a bar that was almost black, the usual crazy glassware behind, BUD in buzzing neon, an ancient jukebox, a handful of tiny tables. Just us and the bartender. "Anything for ya?" he said as he walked in from the harsh, yellow night, blinking at the darkness of the place.

He didn't look like a fag, but I usually can't spot the boys. He was young, which surprised me, with bright red hair, like rust or something. I asked for my usual Bud, and Shelly chipped in a little for a Daniel's on ice. We didn't make a lot of bucks, me working for the print shop and Shelly down at the courthouse, and we couldn't afford much. I remember I got this little stab of pissed-offness—like she either didn't care we were almost broke or was determined to have me pick up the tab for her parting shot.

We sat at one of the little tables for a few minutes and talked the usual bullshit: me about lithography and Quark like they were God's gift to mankind, and her bitching about the drones in the courthouse.

Like I said, I'm not the best kind of person to pick up on stuff, so I didn't know what to say when she said, "I'm going to the can—come with?" I probably just sat there like an idiot as she smiled at me, then turned and walked toward an ugly door marked CAN.

It wasn't really about the sex. I mean, if there was one thing I'd bitch about it was how she really didn't give a flip about money, always buying things when we didn't have a dime. I'd have to pay the rent and find out we had jack in the account because she'd gone off and bought some CDs or something.

Sex was not the problem, at least not until recently when it all started to slide. But that look she flashed at me—that brought me way back, back to when she first moved in, back when we never seemed to have our clothes on.

But thickheaded me, it took a couple of seconds for me to remember that look and hear exactly what she'd said. After it finally sunk in, I got up, almost knocking my chair over onto the floor, and with that red-haired kid watching followed Shelly into the CAN.

✠ ✠ ✠

For a sec I thought she was attacking me or something. I had one foot in the door and wham! she's right there, arms wrapped around me, kissing me like mad. I freaked a little, trying to push back against the door, but she kept right on at me, pushing her little self against me, squishing her little tits against mine. Her tongue pushed past my teeth, pushed against my own. Like I said, I didn't get it at first, but when her hot breath filled my mouth and her tongue really started to work I figured it out.

So there we were, a couple of dykes tongue dancing in the bathroom of the El Rio. It was hot. Did I just say hot? I was fucking melting, man. Shelly had always been a damned good kisser. For a little slip of a thing, with those sly little lips, she knew how to do it right: tongue—oh, yeah—but also with these little playful bites; and she'd rub her tiny nose on my big honker, which always made me giggle like a damn little girl. Good? She was the best.

Then she was at my tits. You could park a bus on my ass, but I really liked my tits. What was great is that Shelly liked them too. Kinda bothered me sometimes, when she'd just sit down in front of me and touch them and touch them and touch them, then lick, then kiss my nipples—like the world had shrunk down to just this little girl and my big boobs. But sometimes, like that time in the CAN of the El Rio, God was in her Heaven, because Shelly's hands went to my shirt, frantically unbuttoned it, and pushed it aside like a curtain to a damn hot show.

I like sports bras, and so does Shelly. She smiled wickedly up at me, eyes shining like polished dimes, as she stroked me through the stretchy stuff. Damn right my nipples were hard, and my cunt was getting wet. I remember I leaned forward, like I was begging for another of those kisses—which I was—but she just kept up that cat-and-cream smile and flipped up my bra, flopping out my tits.

Right then I realized that I was in the CAN of the El Rio. I mean, I knew that, but with Shelly's tongue down my throat I was lucky I could remember my last name, let alone where the fuck I was. It wasn't like we were just necking in my truck or sneaking in a wild quickie on a hillside. This was a sleazy dive that once a year just happened to hang up a queer flag, and we were necking like horny teenagers in the fucking bathroom.

But tell that to Shelly. I don't know what the barkeep put in that Daniel's, but I should buy stock in the company; at least that's what I thought at the time. I wanted to haul her out of there and off to a quiet, dark street in my truck, but all she did was playfully bat my hands away from where I was trying to pull my bra back down, and then she latched her sweet lips onto my right nipple.

Damn, that did it. I knew some girls who look on their tits like they belong to someone else, but not me. I've got one of those nipple-to-cunt hook-ups: Get someone who really knows how to put lips to tit and I'm all off in a fuzzy place just letting the come wash over me.

She knew how to kiss, and she sure as hell knew how to suck tit. Lips, tongue, the whole damn thing right there on my nipple. My legs went all limp and my eyes just plain faded out. Back against the door, I felt myself lose motor control. Shelly smiled around my fat nipple, gave me an evil look, and kept right on sucking. I'm not what you'd call a fast comer, but bam! right then and there I came the fastest I'd ever. I remember it because this little part of my mind thought for a second that I might be having a stroke or something. Then I realized that it was a damn religious experience, and I found myself saying so without realizing it: "Oh, God!"

She quickly shushed me, putting her little hand over my mouth. "Unless you want to have someone else in here," she added in a low, husky voice.

I definitely didn't want that, and shook my head at least once or twice. We kissed, but this time her hands were on my nipple, tugging at me and twisting, just enough, back and forth. Her hot breath mixed with mine, bringing me up to a boiling point. Her other hand was working my crotch, kneading my cunt through the thick denim of my pants. I started to pant down her throat; it was that good. I knew it was that good because I wasn't doing anything by myself. My body was on its own.

Somehow I realized her hand had left my nipple. God knows how long it was until I figured that out, but there you go. I opened my eyes, feeling them pop against the sweat that was almost gluing them shut.

What did I see? Oh, man, it was so tasty. I think about it a lot, even today.

The first thing I thought was that the damn CAN in the El Rio was really a pit: piss-yellow sink (I tried really hard not to think about that), bizarre Jackson Pollock floor (something else not to think about), stalls covered with billions of years of filthy graffiti.

The second was that Shelly had never looked so pretty. There she was, standing close, eyes half shut, one hand on my right tit, one hand up between her legs. That wild gypsy skirt was bunched all up around her waist, and her little hand was working at her hot little quim.

For a long time I just stared down at her. Her mouth was also half-open, her hot breath warming my face. Distantly, I could hear the little slick, slick, slick sounds of her fingers flickering between her legs, over her clit.

I've regretted a lot of crap over the years: all those times when I fucked up, made the bad call. That day I did one that I've kicked myself over ever since, but at least I did one thing right: I kissed her.

Shelly and her kisses. They were always good, but that time in the CAN of the El Rio in Paris, Tex., they were the best they'd ever been. Her hand on my tit, her hand in my cunt, it was the best it could ever be.

We didn't really come together, but we were damn close. Her panting breaths in my mouth pushed me right over the edge, and as I shook and felt my legs get all tense—then loose—I felt her do the same in my arms.

Holding each other up, we panted some more until the blood eased a little out of our cunts and a bit more into our brains. Sniffling and weak as all get-out, we put ourselves together. It felt like hours, but it had probably been only a few minutes.

She kissed me then, leaned forward and planted one right on my cheek. I said I wasn't good at hiding things, and she proved it: "That's the best goodbye I can give."

✠ ✠ ✠

Outside, the red-haired guy just smiled as we limped and stumbled back to our rickety little table. We smiled for a while; then I had to struggle off to the CAN (sex always makes me have to piss). Ever try to take a leak in a place you desperately try not to touch? Try it some time if you really want a challenge.

Like I said, that was the end of it. It might not have been the best call—especially after that time in the bathroom of that pit—but that's the way it was.

The worst thing, though, is that after we broke up I didn't have sex for more than two years.

And Shelly? Shelly married the bartender.

Beer

Tammy Stoner

W e stepped out of the steam-grate-piss-snow Philadelphia streets and into McGlinchey's Bar. I ordered a scotch, straight up to wash down the Drip. She skipped the chaser all together, thinking it melted her edge.

She—the one who dances inside the Bermuda Triangle of me and her two boyfriends, trying to mysteriously disappear. She—the one wanting to melt, not wanting to melt, wanting to melt, not wanting to melt.

I watched her across the alternately slick and sticky pressed wood tabletop, eyes wide, sucking on someone's discarded lime, lighting cigarettes for me. *You stare at me with too much intensity,* she said. *You're more intense than you realize,* she said. *Kiss me,* she said...

When the Glass Blower and his girlfriend Acrylic glided in, she moved from her side of the booth to mine. I felt her muscular thigh brush up against mine. Muscular from obsessive hours of fat draining in tight shirts and loose pants with a handful of laxatives and a callous of a middle finger. *From hitting my front teeth.*

My ex was a stripper. She was never my ex, really, but this one thinks the stripper is my ex because we kissed in front of her…three days before she asked me to kiss her for the first time. *I'm swear I'm ready,* she assured me. The stripper drove her jealous-crazy—not because she stripped but because she enjoyed it completely. Straightedge pole climber. Now I don't see anyone but my Lime Sucker, even though I sleep with strange friends now and again.

Every other night I sit by the phone wondering what reason she'll devise for not being able to visit me. She can get very creative under pressure…

She runs her hand under the table, beelining to my crotch. Addict. The bar is dark. The smoke zapper chars the air above us. Glass Blower orders a pitcher of Rolling Rock for him and his girlfriend. My girlfriend nods when he asks if she'd like a glass for herself, fingers rubbing me in tiny circles, feeling wetness through my wool pants. Wool pants and a T-shirt. I told her, *I don't trust the weatherman.*

"But what if you get too hot?" she asked.

"I'll cut the pants off."

"Too cold?"

"I'll borrow your sweater."

But I know she'd never give me her sweater, not until she loses 10 more pounds. *From where?* I ask. *From here,* she says, pinching a flap of skin from her midsection. *Not from here?* I ask, looking up at her as I bite her nipples…

Someone puts more rock and roll on the jukebox behind us, complaining bitterly that AC/DC had more songs than just

"Back in Black" and "You Shook Me All Night Long." Her fingers press harder. I spread my legs to make room, worried my face might be flushing because the Glass Blower can always sniff out sex. Fortunately he's too involved in chatter with his lady and her friend, the bald waitress with a rosary tattooed on her upper arm.

I can smell her perfume more strongly now. It always dances around me when she's turned on. I want to touch her, too, being jerked off like this makes me feel slightly self-conscious. Stage fright.

She pushes two fingers down my wet line as far as they will go, teasing me. I want her to push inside me. *Fuck me.*

The waitress drops off their beer. Acrylic pours for my girl, looking a little too deeply into her eyes. She knows she's with me. *Besides, you're straight, right?* She removes her hand to grab the beer and flirt a little with Acrylic until I stand up abruptly and go to the bathroom. Glare at her for flirting in front of me. Again.

Two seconds later she's pounding on the faded green door. I let her in, but before I can say a word she throws me up against the wall, holds my arms above my head and kisses me. Hard. Moaning. It's so unusual for her to take direct control that I'm thrown back and don't respond at first. She jerks away, hurt.

"What?" I say, too loudly. "I'm just startled...don't stop..."

My girl's only gone down on me once before, holding me like a chalice. It threw her into another 12 rounds of denial, so I never let her do it again. But now I have no choice. There is no stopping.

She drops to her knees on the damp, ashy floor under a buzzing lightbulb and unzips my pants. I want to touch her, but she won't allow it. I lean back and remember tugging on her nipples last week, her screaming out so loudly I had to cover her face with a pillow. The Vietnamese neighbors banging on the wall.

I apologized the next day for being so rough. *No,* she whispered into her work phone, *the pain makes me think about you all day.*

Now she slams her face hungrily into me, smearing her lipstick as sucks me off, her hands spreading me as far open as I'll go. I feel heat rise into my stomach and down my legs. She flicks her surprisingly confident tongue up and down until I arch into her, begging her to go harder. Instead, she pulls back and touches me with the very tip of her tongue until I'm crazy. Light feathery touches almost too soft to feel. I focus. She's the only thing in my world. I try to grab on to the soft slow movement, but I can't. I need more.

Someone knocks at the door. She dives back into me, moving her hot tongue around and around until my legs shake. My heart beats in my ears. My pants soak up the excess and I come in three waves, my tailbone banging the wall with each jerk. She smiles, washes her hands then kisses me on the neck.

"We'll be right out," she singsongs. The bathroom reeks of her perfume and mine. I start to draw a cartoon of us on the wall, but she stops me. Says her boyfriend's band plays here. "Don't, he knows your style."

"He doesn't know me."

"He studies you." She reaches inside my pocket and pulls out a cigarette to light for me. I brush off a few pieces of overprocessed, bleached hairs from her black sweater.

"Why does he study me?" I ask.

"Because he knows…" her eyes blaze into me.

"Knows what?" I push, again.

"He knows how I feel…"

"How do you feel?" I ask, taking the Camel from her thin hands.

"I…I feel like a beer," she laughs weakly, opening the door.

I followed her back to the booth, bumping through the crowds. Glass Blower sniffed out a knowing laugh as we sat back down, then kissed Acrylic on the back of the neck, one dark eye watching us. Throbbing.

I poured my Lime Sucker a glass of warm beer that she never finished, taking only small sips until she finally left it behind.

In Harm's Way

ROSALIND CHRISTINE LLOYD

Traveling is one of my passions. Being an airline employee for almost five years permits me to be a low-budget jet setter. My road partner, Ted, works with me in the international lounge for a major airline at JFK airport in New York City. Ted is a Cartier-obsessed glamour boy, the body-beautiful gentleman's man, soul brother number one. I'm a self-indulging, holistically New Age, semipolitical, Afrocentric, down-by-law, woman-obsessed, androgynous femme, with tastes ranging from the highly delicate, feminine-aggressive personality to the rock-hard, bull-dyke submissive. In other words, I consider myself a well-guided, heat-seeking missile Scorpion. Together, Ted and I scour cities both big and small in search of what we refer to as "stimulating revelations."

This particular trip took us to Amsterdam, the land of coffeehouses, canals, Van Gogh, windmills, tulips, and what I call the big four H's: Heineken, Hashish, the Hague, and legal rights for Homosexuals. I was so excited that after a visit to the sex and tattoo museums, I decided this would be where I would bravely experience my first tattoo.

After exploring a fair share of Amsterdam's shops and open-air markets, Ted and I did some architectural sightseeing. Ted had been to Amsterdam many times and was the perfect guide. Touring the impressive 17th-century mansions and town houses, I could not help marveling at the array of rainbow-colored flags adorning establishments throughout the city. The flags flew over bars, bookstores, cafés, restaurants, and boutiques. Without issue, two women walked by in a loving embrace, strolling the bank of the canal along the cobblestone street. The element was quite free and compelling. I felt right at home.

We came to one gay flag waving above a rather inviting bar. Ted suggested we go in. This particular establishment happened to be one of the few lesbian bars in the city, Vive la Reine.

Since it was early afternoon, there was only a small group of women having an animated conversation in their native tongue. Although Amsterdam is a Dutch-speaking city, almost everyone also speaks English. Ted and I sat at the bar and ordered a couple of Heinekens. The bartender was attentive and quite pretty. After telling her we were Americans and that it was my first visit to the Netherlands, I mentioned I was impressed by the displays at the tattoo museum and that I was eager to get my first tattoo while on vacation. I asked her if she knew of a safe and reliable parlor.

"Oh, for sure," she answered in slangy Dutch-accented English, rolling up one of her sleeves to reveal a magnificent tattoo of two mermaids intertwined in an aquatic 69 on her upper right arm.

"It's beautiful," I remarked, amazed at its vibrance against her skin.

"My lover and I have a matching set. We've had them as long as we've been together. Let me tell you where you must go. It is a place called the Psychedelic Scar. It is over on Reguliersdwarsstr. Speak to a girl called Pagan. She is bald with a dragon tattooed on her head and a tusk of ivory in her septum. She is clean and by far the most experienced artist there."

Walking from Vive, we decided I would get my tattoo tomorrow night, but on this night we would get dressed up and do some men's clubs so Ted could "get his freak on."

My kinky hair, full of springy spirals, was wild and untamed all over my head. Wearing my hair like this makes me feel recklessly treacherous. My juicy lips were painted a delicious shade of chocolate. I dotted scented oil on my erogenous zones. The outfit I chose made my agenda only that more obvious. A tight black Lycra top with a wide-open neck showed skin and gave my breasts a nice in-your-face presentation. The black suede collar with rhinestones was one of my favorite "fun" pieces I like to call my "pussy collar." My levitating platform boots and black vinyl jeans that remind me of shiny shower curtains finished the look, underneath my overly feminine cropped leather jacket. Meeting in the hotel lobby, Ted looked at me before glancing down at his tight Levi's and white T-shirt and saying, "Is it you or me tricking tonight, Ms. Girl?"

The Inferno is a popular mixed club where anything goes. The line to get in is unforgiving because the place is full of drama-loving drag queens, naked muscle boys, and European trisexual girls, thrown in with a mixture of everything else you can imagine. You are almost guaranteed a mad time.

After a 15-minute wait, we were finally inside, welcomed by a deep house beat that moved Ted.

"Oh, Trina, isn't this place fabulous! Every time I come here I have a good time!" he shouted over the music.

"Honey, I can see why it's crazy in here," I agreed while glancing at a group of gender-confusing people throwing a private party in public. Barring whatever aspects of the performance that did not appeal to you, it was quite daring, a voyeuristic feast for the eyes and imagination, as girls clung to boys that clung to boys that clung to girls that clung to girls dancing together in a (fully clothed) frenzied orgy of affection.

Ted ordered drinks and we made a toast.

"Here's to the Dutch!" Ted's eyes were glazed over, his brown cheeks beginning to burn.

"The Dutch!" I repeated, clicking his glass and swallowing the contents of mine. That's when I felt it: the unmistakable heat of a stare. The Inferno was very dark, lit only by a carnival of neon, strobe, and laser beams. Through the darkness, her presence, under a solitary spotlight, was undeniable. She had skin the color of gingerbread, and her face had a fine and dignified bone structure. Her eyes, framed with a thick fringe of lashes, were unusually dark, with what seemed an endless depth. Her mouth was the most sensuous I have ever seen, lips longing to be lecherously lingered upon. Standing at the far end of the bar, she posed with one foot poised on a bar stool, adorned in stylishly handsome, handmade black leather boots. The black leather halter top was beguiling, taming two voluminous globes of feminine flesh like sugar cones struggling to contain two scoops of coffee-flavored Häagen-Dazs. Her leather pants seemed designed to caress her every dimension with the high quality of tailored perfection. Her shiny, long black hair was pulled back in a ponytail, falling down her back in dramatic waves—like the waves of the Sargasso Sea at midnight.

While I embraced her vision, her mesmerizing eyes stared back at me with an almost corrupt expression that compelled me to look away.

After Ted finished his drink, a big, beautiful black Dutchman, about 6 feet 5 inches and 250 pounds, approached him, hugging

Ted very affectionately. Although it was unclear whether Ted actually knew him, this didn't seem to matter because Ted shouted to me, "See you later, girl," as the man whisked him to the dance floor.

There was a tap on my shoulder. It was the bartender.

"This is compliments of the lady." Before me was a strange-looking cocktail, a double shot of a dark reddish-brown liquor lit by a blue flame. Taking a deep breath, I turned to meet Leather's gaze. She had an identical drink in her hands. When our eyes met she raised her glass in my honor. With one strong puff, she blew out the flame before knocking the contents of her glass to the back of her throat. I looked to the bartender for help.

"It is called a *flamagger*. Here." He placed a straw inside the glass, carefully laying it against the inside edge. "Be careful not to let the straw catch the flame. Just quickly suck on it before it gets too hot," he advised.

Mindfully following his instructions, I did precisely that, treated to a mild blast of the flame at the end of the suck that ignited something within me. I turned around to thank Leather, but she was already heading in my direction. To say she was a sight to behold is an understatement. Her strong, well-sculpted body was decorated in dramatic tribal tattoos that covered her creamy brown skin. A tattoo vine of ivy starting from the nape of her neck wrapped itself around toward the other side of her chest, ending short of her cleavage. An identical bracelet of ivy surrounded her left wrist. An unidentifiable brand mark adorned the inside of her right wrist. A black panther clawed its way down her right arm. Each of her ears was pierced with five tiny gold hoops. As she walked, her breasts seemed heavy, and those long legs in those leather pants were making me crazy. As she grew near, I spotted a moderate-size bulge against her left inner thigh. Exasperated, I started to tremble, trying to suppress my arousal while maintaining my cool. She came right up to me, standing so close I could smell the mixture of leather, perspiration, and body lotion all at once. Her body heat was searing.

"So, you like *flamaggers*?" Her voice was deep and raspy, her Dutch accent heavy.

"Flame—oh, the drink! Yes, yes. It was my first ever. Thank you." I was a nervous wreck just standing near her. Her beauty was shocking, and her leather was dangerously appealing.

"Let's have another," she said. The bartender had already set up two more. Closing one eye, Leather lit a cigarette, letting it hang from the corner of her lip. "My name is Harmony. But I go by Harm. You must call me Harm."

I shivered when she said it. As she gave some Dutch money to the bartender, her free hand had taken my hand, raising it to her face, gently guiding it to caress her cheek, my hand just inches away from the fiery tip of the cigarette in her mouth.

"I'm Trina—short for Christine," I responded, cringing from the tiny dot of heat from her cigarette.

"Trina." She said it with rolling R's. "I like the way your name feels on my tongue," she added, giving me a modest glimpse of the piercing that adorned her tongue. No surprise there.

"Please, have your shot." She whispered this, moving closer to me, her hands now caressing my hips, the heat of her thigh pressing against me. Gently, she placed the straw between my lips, telling me to suck, and I did without a hint of resistance. After that, Harm lit a blunt joint of hashish with the most bountiful aroma. This signaled the beginning of the end.

I usually resist this type of aggressive female posturing back home. More provocative in my pursuits, I thrill at proposing the most compelling of challenges—in other words, women must earn my submission. But in this exotically foreign country, I found this particular scenario precariously alluring. Besides, I obviously underestimated the power of *flamaggers*. After the third, we were back in a dark corner of the club. I ached as Harm's rock-hard body pressed against me, her breath hot from liquor, cigarette smoke, and God only knows what else, thick in her kiss. Her tongue felt soft and slippery, and she maneuvered her piercing around my mouth and tongue like a divine protrusion. I was melting, my back arched as she went underneath my top, spreading her hands like wings, surrounding the small of my back. I froze at the sensation of her hands against my skin, one in particular now mysteriously sheathed in superthin, well-moisturized black rubber gloves.

As I was too overwhelmed with lust to protest, my arousal amplified when her long, thick fingers found their way to my buttocks. In a few swift maneuvers, she opened my shiny vinyl pants and slid her hands inside. Gently, she rubbed my bottom with an increasing intensity that escalated into aggressive groping. Traveling lower, she concentrated on the rim of my anus with the tip of her rubber-covered finger tracing circles round and round and round. Within my next heartbeat, Harm had rammed her finger into my ass while roughly whispering unintelligible things into my ear, an act that propelled me into a powerful spasm. Covering my mouth with hers, now hot like fire, she seized the opportunity to push her finger even deeper inside me. My ass hungrily swallowing her finger, I knew I was dying from the strength and persistence of my spasms, but the hashish haze carried me to the throes of ecstasy, leaving me desperate for more.

Slowly, she pulled her finger from inside me, removing her glove, turning it inside out, and stuffing it deep inside her back pocket before gently guiding me back to the bar, summoning the bartender for another round. After what had just happened, I knew I would neither be smoking any more hash nor having another shot.

Ted returned to check on me. All he could do was stare—first at me, then at Harm, and back at me again.

"Ted, this is Harmony, and Harmony, this is my best friend, Ted." My voice was reduced to a breathy wilt; neither of them paid it any attention.

"Harm," Leather corrected. "Good to meet you, Ted. I like your friend, Trina. Bartender, give Ted a drink on me, would you, darling?"

"Ooh, Trina, I like her already!" Ted teased, carefully eyeing Harmony's outfit and demeanor. All I could do was stand there and smile stupidly, still feeling Harmony inside me and very open for what was to come. The hash had both mellowed me out and opened me up. Ted collected his scotch and soda and left.

"This toast is to Harm!" she said slickly, raising her glass in the air, taking the straw from my glass and handing me the torched beverage.

"I don't think I can handle another."

"Oh, but you must. You must drink. Let me show you all the good things Amsterdam has to offer, Trina." Harm pushed the drink toward my lips; we blew simultaneously and swallowed. My head seemed lighter than a feather, and my entire body felt the rush of a bushfire. Before I knew it, Harmony and I were on the massively crowded dance floor. Holding me so close I could barely breathe, the hard knot against her thigh inside her leather pants pressed deep into me until I felt bruised. One of her hands crushed me to her, while the other manipulated one of my nipples between her fingers, pinching it so hard I thought I would faint. My inner core was vibrating to the point where my soul was begging Harm for it. Placing both of her hands on top of my head, Harmony pushed me toward the floor until I was in a kneeling position directly opposite her crotch. As she mashed herself into my face, I grabbed her thighs and kissed her cock with total submission, feeling myself coming again, fast and hard, succumbing to the burning, tingling sensation in my bottom. The longer I kissed her, the more my desire increased for the taste of leather, the taste of her, the arch of her cock in my mouth, and the filling-up of my ass. She soon took to banging herself into my face. I fell in love.

I felt an urgent tap on my shoulder, which was difficult to acknowledge, as Harmony had both of her hands on either side of my head and was feeding herself to my hungry mouth. I allowed myself a moment to peek up at Ted, who was flanked by a small, adoring audience that had assembled in our honor.

"Ah, Trina, do you have a minute?" he whispered. I looked up at Harm. She had already moved to light a cigarette, dismissing me. I was far too drunk to be embarrassed. Ted helped me up, to a resounding round of applause. All I could do was a curtsy regally as we exited the club.

"Ms. Thing, have you lost your mind?" he hollered humorously. The moon was full, Ted was drunk, and I was totally aroused.

"Ted, I think I did lose my mind, so we better go get that tattoo before I find it."

Hangin' Around

RANDENTRASHINACANN

It was an ordinary cold summer day in San Francisco. I was called in to set up lighting for the Dina Lounge dance club. I showed up a bit late (fag time, you know) to the buzzing sounds of last-minute fury.

I walked up the back stairs to the small black overhang jutting out in the shadows high above the floor. There was just enough room for a worktable and maybe three techs and their equipment. As I strapped on my tool belt, Adam told me we needed help with the lights, but we didn't have any ladders. Being a lover of heights and just a bit crazy, I agreed to scale the beams from the balcony strip.

A few minutes later I re-aimed the lights to hit the stage,

then asked for some plastic gels from our new technical assistant who was busy cutting them in the balcony work area. The look on her face said *Come and get them yourself,* so I shimmied over.

I watched her facial expression change as I wrapped my legs and right arm upside down around the beam and arched back to reach the gels with my free hand. "I like that position!" she said, snatching them out of my reach.

"Fuck you!" I yelled playfully. "Give me those gels!"

"I'll do both," she replied, "if you promise to come right back." She had a tough-girl shaved head. Dark eyes. Ragged T-shirt with a sweatshirt wrapped around her waist.

"Don't be a tease," I said.

"If there's one thing I'm not, it's a tease."

"Then I'll be back later."

"I'll be waiting." She sounded so serious.

I grabbed the gels and went back to finish the job, *quickly.* By now the bartenders were Windexing and buffing far below, telling delivery boys where to stack their cases of booze. Someone clicked on a vacuum cleaner.

As I slid in the last gel frame, I looked back to see if the new tech assistant was still watching, but I couldn't see in the blinding glare of the lights. My cunt was throbbing—partly from humping the beams, and partly from the thought of the hot sex I could have hanging off one. I had to slide back and see if she was still there.

This time I scooted all the way into the work area, where she stood below, fixing an old par can at the worktable. I swung my feet down, accidentally hitting her in the back of the head with my boot. She spun around, grabbed both my ankles, and mischievously roped them together. She then stood up on the table, flipped my body forward, and handcuffed my wrists between my legs so I was draped face down over the beam. Hog-tied.

"Now who's gonna fuck you?" she scoffed, watching me struggle while she latched the small door.

She duct taped my mouth shut. I felt my clit swell. The blood rushed to my head, and I thought I would get off just watching the intensity in her eyes.

Then I realized where I'd seen her before. She came to a meeting the Dina Lounge held a few months back to orient the tech crew, only her hair was longer and red. I thought she was hot, but I had my jealous girlfriend (now ex) on my arm, so I avoided her. She'd tried to strike up conversation a few times, but I was worried my girlfriend might think I was flirting (which I would have been), so I blew her off.

"Be still!" she commanded, pulling a utility knife out of her pocket. She cut a careful line down the back seam of my pants and ripped them open, exposing my bare pussy and ass. She grabbed the cord of the disassembled par can, splayed the wires and began whipping my ass. The tips of the wires were exposed, giving a sweet, sharp sting and a bit of a scratch with every whack. I was entering euphoria rapidly when the DJ started playing below us, and I looked down to see more people entering the club. She smacked my ass again. I thought the people could see us if they looked up. That notion took me to another level.

Seeing my distraction, she changed her aim from my ass to my pussy, spreading my thighs apart with her hand while probing my ass with her little finger. She stopped just before I was about to come, smiled at me, and jumped down off the table. She rummaged through her tools for a pair of latex work gloves, a screwdriver and a big-ass pair of bolt cutters. After tying the par can chord tightly around my neck, she hopped back onto the table, covered the screwdriver handle with one of the gloves, and shoved it into my ass.

The second glove barely fit over the bolt-cutter head. I gasped as she worked it slowly into my throbbing cunt. Small, steady movements in and out rubbed just the right spot as heat spread like fire up my groin into my head. It already felt like she would rip me open; then she flicked the safety latch, and the tension from the spring took me the rest of the way there. Fluids streamed from my eyes and cunt as she squeezed and opened the cutters.

She abruptly stopped and removed them slowly, teasing me all the way. After unlocking the cuffs, she grabbed the cord around my neck and pulled me toward her to restrict my breathing. She balled her hand and pushed into me.

I felt my cunt open to swallow her fist. She fucked me so hard I almost passed out, fist banging against the tender spots deep inside me as I came. I felt my juices run down the legs of my shredded work pants. Slowly, very slowly, she pulled out. I felt myself contract and relax again.

While I balanced there in a shaking heap over the beam, she hopped down to gather the tools that had fallen from my tool belt. Laying them on the table, she ripped the tape from my mouth, untied my sleeping ankles, and uncuffed my sore wrists. I managed to compose myself enough to climb down, my face still flushed. She lit a cigarette, blowing a cocky stream of smoke my way. I was covered in sweat, dirt from the beam, and dripping with jism; I wondered how I could discreetly leave the club in this condition.

"What's your name?" she asked, removing her sweatshirt and tying it around my waist to camouflage my damaged, wet pants.

"I'm Trash," I replied, taking a drag from her cigarette.

"I'm Scrappy," she offered, and helped me down from the table. She pulled the pussy-covered gloves from her tools and threw them down at the crowd below. I smirked, "Nice!" Then we walked together out of the tech room, down the stairs and to the front door of the club.

"Nice working with you," she said, shaking my still trembling hand. "We'll have to do it again sometime." We left, walking in separate directions, and never crossed paths again. But I will never forget the night I spent *hanging around* at the Dina Lounge.

Piss Off

JULIA PRICE

It was retro-punk night at the Warehouse, Lincoln's only dyke club. Twenty-something girls were dressed to the nines with their hair sprayed blue, their breasts and bellies hanging out of torn T-shirts, their asses out of plaid bondage pants and ripped-up jeans, and their short school-girl skirts rolled up. And you looking like you don't give a damn about your bad reputation.

You followed me into the bathroom; what made you do that? Had you noticed how I'd been watching you all night, chain-smoking as I tried not to let you see that I was looking, wondering, wanting?

I was sitting on my bar stool, ordering drink after drink,

noticing how good you looked on the threadbare sofa across the empty dance floor. Noticing you in your incredibly short skirt with SEX PISTOLS spray-painted across the ass and hot knee-high lace-up work boots. God, I couldn't take my eyes off of you; you'd have to be clueless not to notice. There were only 15 or 20 of us in the club—and most of them seemed to be friends of the band.

The band, a shitty tattered trio from Seattle, was too loud to talk over, so I never bothered walking over to you—but I think you knew I was watching you. We were both bored. It was late and we were both probably drunk—at least, I know I was. Drunk enough to be horny, at least. Maybe even a little drunker than that.

I stumbled into the restroom, wrinkling my nose at the mingled scents of mold, cheap perfume, and piss. Was the door to the stall really broken, or was I just too drunk to figure out how to close it? Or was it just that I didn't *want* the door closed while I pulled down my black stretch jeans to the tops of my boots—nothing underneath because you get panty lines in stretch jeans—and sat down to piss.

You know how when you're drunk, sometimes it takes a while to piss? It gets worse when you're preoccupied with a girl. So there I sat, in the stink and the swirl of terrible music, my head swimming with beer, my cunt aching with thoughts of you.

I almost believed you were a dream when you appeared in the open door of the stall, short skirt askew, nipples hard and poking out at me plainly like crooked fingers through the white cotton that read STOP STARING AT MY TITS.

I stopped staring at your tits. I looked instead at your legs, then your hips in that tight skirt, then up to your face, your cocky drunken smile and bloodshot eyes. Your eyes drifted from my face to my bare pussy, as I realized I'd drunkenly let my legs drift open while waiting for the piss to come.

I didn't close them.

Then you were on me, pulling up your skirt, sitting down on my lap, facing me. You had this playful look on your face like I was your twin sister and we were just horsing around. I felt your lips on mine, smelled your sweat and the incense on your clothes, sharp with musk and sandalwood, jasmine and rose. That's when my pussy relaxed and the stream came. I felt myself releasing as your tongue wormed its way into my mouth and your chest pressed through your hostile T-shirt to rub against my own. I felt your nipples brush against me as you positioned yourself with your crotch above mine. Your piss hit the toilet with mine. That made me laugh, and I jiggled as I did; suddenly feeling the hot stream of your piss on my pussy. It didn't bother me nearly as much as I thought it would. In fact, I drunkenly snuggled a little closer, droplets scattering across my cunt, soaking my pubic hair. I sighed into your mouth as you finished pissing—and that's when I realized you were touching yourself.

Your hand worked fervently, and it just seemed natural to let my own join in—my fingers on my cunt, now slick with your piss. I found my clit, feeling it harder than ever before, and started to rub. The sensations flooded through me as I rubbed faster. You kissed me hard as you stroked yourself, and then you pulled up your shirt.

I took one of your hard nipples in my mouth, suckling on it while I rubbed my clit in ever-tighter circles, faster and faster. I realized I was going to come. But you beat me, your body jerking and spasming as you climaxed on top of me, your fluid dribbling on me like your piss had done a moment before.

You finished your orgasm and pulled me close, stroking my wiry blood-red crew cut with one hand while I rubbed myself. With your other hand, you reached under my T-shirt and felt my tits. You stroked me, gently pinched my nipples, and kissed me. And when I came, you put your arms around me and gripped me close in an almost desperate gesture of utter and unexpected tenderness like nothing I'd ever felt before.

You held me afterward too, even as the few club chicks wandered into the restroom to find the only stall occupied. We ignored them when they looked in at us. Let them piss in the sink.

Later, when the music ground down into nothing, we were still sitting there holding each other, our ears ringing in the silence. I looked up at you wondering if this was it, if this was all there was going to be between two people. As if in answer, you kissed me gently, stood up, and pulled your skirt down.

You looked back at me once, just outside the stall. A little smile played across your face—subtly wistful…goodbye.

When I left the toilet five minutes later, you were nowhere to be found. I sat on the couch where I'd first seen you and smoked as the band cleaned up, wondering whether you'd left alone.

CLUBLAND

Galatea

VIOLET TAYLOR

I was so nervous that I clutched Jordan's hand desperately as we waited in line to get into the Garage.

"I love holding hands with you," she whispered in my ear. "But if we're holding hands, nobody's going to want to pick you up."

"Right," I said, letting go and wiping my sweaty palm on my skirt. I found myself panicking, wishing I could just go home and let Jordan do her thing at the club, the same thing she did a lot—or better yet, that I could take my beautiful girlfriend home and *we* could fuck, and I wouldn't have to go through this. Jordan was prettier than me, that's why she always went home with someone—well, not always, but that's the way it seemed—and she looked incredible tonight. She wore a little black dress barely concealing that fantastic body of hers, knee-high Doc Martens, long black hair flowing past her white shoulders, her face all made up with blood-red lipstick and pale foundation. She looked like the goth girl of my dreams, which she was, but that wasn't why we were here.

We'd spent months negotiating this—years, if you counted everything that had led up to it. Jordan felt strongly about having a polyamorous relationship, and even though I'd resisted at first, I had to admit the idea did appeal to me. But I was shy, and Jordan was…well, she was what she was. I didn't like to say she was a slut, because it pleased her too much. But she didn't have the insecurities that made it so hard for me to flirt, the weird guilt complex that made it so hard for me to come on to a woman. That had been the main problem in our year of polyamory so far—I wasn't jealous so much because other women were having her but because she was having other women, and she seemed to do it so effortlessly, almost without knowing she was doing it. Oh, I'll admit when it started I felt a little strange knowing that when Jordan dressed up to go out to the clubs with her friends on Friday evening that she was probably not going to be back until morning. That she would probably end the morning tangled in sweaty sheets with some sexy club girl or butch dyke—or, knowing Jordan, maybe even a couple of them. But we worked out a system to keep me from being jealous—every time she came home from her adventures, she'd tell me every detail. I had been reluctant to try that at first, but Jordan swore it had worked with her old girlfriend Kirsten.

The first couple of times we'd tried it, I had felt jealous but managed to hide it enough to let Jordan get through the story. And the way Jordan told a story—complete with tastes, smells, textures, sounds, and emotions—was enough to make me feel like I'd really been there with her. Her storytelling never failed to turn me on.

I was as free as she was, as far as our negotiation went. But I just couldn't do it the way she could—not that I didn't want to or anything; there were plenty of women I was attracted to. I just felt so self-conscious, and women didn't come on to me or at least, that's what *I* thought. Jordan teased me that they came on to me all the time and I was just too clueless to notice.

My jealousy about Jordan's exploits led to endless hours of processing in bed after she'd told me her stories (and, once I got a little more comfortable, after we'd made love fervently at the stories' conclusions). It was during one of those sessions that I had made what had started out as a joke.

"Why can't *you* take me out and get me laid?" I'd asked her.

And Jordan, with all the enthusiasm of a mother about to pimp out her 16-year-old daughter, had shrieked in delight. "You really mean it? You'd let me do that?"

"You'd really do that?"

"You'd really *let* me do that?"

"Of course I'd let you do that," I said, too quickly. "But it would never work. I'm not the kind of woman other women pick up."

"You are *not* going to start telling me you're not sexy again, are you?"

"Well…I'm not sexy in that way."

"You mean they think you're straight?"

"Sometimes," I said. "But no, I just don't appeal to the kind of women who pick women up, you know? I just think it's something about my style. You're so cool. I'm just kind of… normal."

"Honey," said Jordan, "*normal* is the easiest thing in the world to fix."

That's how the makeover had started, like *My Fair Lady* meets *Reform School Girls*. At first Jordan just wanted to dress me up like a club slut; then she wanted to teach me how to dance. I've never been a good dancer, which is why I never go to dance clubs; I just get embarrassed. But Jordan showed me everything she knew, and when I proved too embarrassed to dance to the highly charged Nine Inch Nails even in the living room of our West Hollywood cottage, for fear the wind might blow the curtains and the neighbors might see me making a fool out of myself, Jordan fixed everything: She got me drunk. Margaritas at first, then straight tequila when it became obvious that there was more teaching necessary than even Jordan had envisioned and it became a pain in the ass to make three pitchers of margaritas just to get me to dance to top-volume DJ Shadow in the middle of the living room.

"Tequila is good for you," Jordan said the first time she held out a lime for me. "It's so incredibly sexual. Lick my hand, drink the shot, stick the lime in your mouth, and suck it."

I licked the salt off Jordan's hand, downed the drink, shuddered as I crammed the lime into my mouth.

Jordan waited a moment as the warmth of the tequila went through me.

"Isn't your pussy getting wet?"

"No!" I said, talking around the lime.

"Oh, come on, not just a little bit?"

I thought about it. We were both sitting there in the living room in our underwear, Jordan looking fetching in a black T-shirt and biking shorts, me wearing a white tank top and boxers. Both of us we wearing running shoes.

"Not even a little bit?" she asked.

"No."

"Maybe tequila just doesn't do it to you. Wait, let me check," said Jordan, slipping her hand up the leg of my boxers. "Hey! You liar!"

I blushed bright red.

"See? Drink more tequila," she said, looking like she was going to kiss me. "Have three more shots, and then it's time to dance."

I sighed. "Do I have to have three?"

"Yes, damn it," said Jordan. "Remember what I told you

about your hips last night. I want to see you put that into practice tonight, understand?"

"Um…maybe we'd better make it four, then," I said, feeling my face flush hot, and not just from the tequila.

Jordan poured.

It had gone on like that for something like three months, every weekend and most weeknights. Jordan was a consummate dirty dancer—I'd seen her on the dance floor, and she could seduce the entire room before the chorus of "Closer." She taught me how to use my hips, my eyes, my lips, my tits, even how to spread my legs and not look like I was doing it. If she hadn't gotten me drunk, I never would have learned a thing.

"Only one thing, though," she told me once, "you can't get drunk when you actually do it."

"Oh, fuck. Why?"

"I'm not sure why. You just…well, it's no fun if you're totally fucked up."

"Just a few drinks?"

"One. Maybe two. But they have to be tequila shots."

"Why?"

Jordan licked her hand, downed her shot, sucked the lime, a sensuous shudder going through her body as the taste of the tequila hit her. She looked at me, her lips curved around the rind of the lime, and I was immediately seized with the desire to take off what little clothes she was wearing.

"See?" she said, her mouth full.

"All right," I said. "You've convinced me."

Jordan also showed me how to dress—not to dress like her, mind you, because I could never manage that with a straight face, but to dress like an overly sexy version of myself. I had a little money saved, and Jordan pitched in some, and we bought me some leather pants, a few little baby tees, and high lace-up boots. I had wanted to buy motorcycle boots, but Jordan said they were a bitch to dance in—lace-ups were bad enough, but eminently sexy. Toward the end of the process she made me get all dressed up, put on makeup and everything, and dance without getting drunk. By then I was even able to do it without blushing—even the sexiest, most overt moves Jordan had shown me.

"Fantastic!" she shrieked, clapping as she watched me. "I want to rip your clothes off and fuck you right now!"

"Yeah, but you're my girlfriend," I said.

"That's right. And I thank Providence every time you dance like that."

That made me blush.

We'd decided on a particular Saturday night to go to Fuel, a local dance party for women, because it was a week after our anniversary. At that point Jordan hadn't gone to the clubs in several months, forgoing her clubbing to teach me the ins and outs of being a club slut. When, a couple of days before Fuel, she suggested casually that I might look cuter and dykier with a different haircut, I was the one who suggested cutting it all off. I'd had long red hair since I was a little girl, and always been very attached to it, but somewhere in the process of learning to dress and dance, I'd lost interest. Jordan stayed sober that night, but I needed more than a few shots to get me to sit in that chair.

I even cried a little as I watched it falling away, but there was something hot about the transformation. I was nude as Jordan sheared me, and I felt this sense of surrender, of giving myself over to the lifestyle Jordan liked so much—not least because it excited me too. When she had my hair down to less than a half-inch, she brought out the burgundy hair dye.

"Are you serious?" I asked her.

"Only if you are," she said, and I nodded.

✠ ✠ ✠

So here I was inside the club, standing amid hundreds of women my own age and younger, dressed in everything from white spandex minidresses to black jeans and Harley Davidson T-shirts. I could smell the girl sweat and it made me dizzy.

"Two shots," Jordan told me. "Then you've got to ask some pretty girl to dance."

She saw me go pale. "Three shots," she laughed, and waved the bartender over.

Jordan made me suck the salt off my own hand this time, "So people won't think we're together."

"Fuck you," I smiled.

"No, that's tomorrow night. When you tell me all about the great time you had."

I did the shot, sucked the lime, and looked around. I found myself looking at a cute blond girl dressed in jeans and a Goldschlager tank top. Jordan followed my gaze and leaned over to whisper in my ear.

"That's Josie," Jordan whispered. "Everyone's had her."

"Jordan!" I snapped at her.

She shrugged. "Just telling it like it is," she told me. "She's not too bad."

"So *you've* had her?"

"Three times," said Jordan. "And don't you *dare* start getting jealous, Violet. This is about you and your newfound slut status, remember?"

"You just met her here and fucked her three times?"

"I know her from school, but they don't allow sex in the classrooms," she said.

Steaming, I poured salt, licked, took my second shot, sucked the lime.

"You should ask her to dance," said Jordan. "She'll say yes. You look fantastic."

"I don't want to sleep with someone everyone's had."

"Who said anything about sleeping with her? You're here to dance, remember?"

I glared at her.

"She's looking over here."

"You've got to be fucking kidding." I kept my back turned away from the girl.

"She's totally checking you out."

"Do *not* look back at her."

"Why not?" Jordan did, and smiled and lifted her eyebrows.

"Jordan! Stop that!"

"She's coming over here."

"Oh, fuck. Oh, fuck. Oh, fuck."

"Hey, Jordan!" said the girl, putting her arms around Jordan and kissing her on the lips. "Still got a beautiful woman on your arm, I see."

"Josie, this is, uh…Monique," said Jordan. "She's new here."

"Pleased to meet you," said Josie, shaking hands and pulling me closer. "Very, very pleased to meet you."

"Likewise," I said, reddening.

Josie stared at me with obvious interest. I had to admit she was cute as hell, with little elfin features and a lip ring, and I could tell she had a nice body packed into those jeans and that tight top without a bra underneath, the rings in her nipples showing plainly through. But she had a sleazy quality I detested; it made my skin crawl.

"Are you two together, or would you care to dance, Monique?"

"Monique needs to have a couple more drinks first," said Jordan, waving at the bartender for refills. "Keep 'em coming," she shouted. "Come sit with us a minute," she told Josie.

"With pleasure," came the response, and I shot Jordan a dirty look.

Somebody Josie knew walked by—it seemed like she knew everybody here, yuck—and she was distracted for a minute while I bent close to Jordan and asked why the hell she told her my name was Monique.

"I might have mentioned you," she whispered back. "I

don't want her to know you're my girlfriend. She might not want to…"

"Want to what?" I hissed.

"Dance with you."

"Don't give me that shit. You want me to sleep with her!"

Jordan shrugged. "She's a great kisser."

"And you *might* have mentioned me?"

"Lighten up. She's a great dancer."

Josie turned back to us.

The tequila arrived while Jordan and Josie chatted about their photography class last semester. I poured salt on my hand.

"Now remember what I told you about drinking tequila," Jordan teased playfully.

Fuck it. I was sick of this, and I wanted to go home. But I thought as long as I was here, I might as well have a little fun, maybe piss Jordan off—put everything she'd taught me into practice.

I turned toward Josie, staring right at her with a smile on my face while I licked, poured more salt, licked some more, aware the whole time that she was watching my tongue with unconcealed interest. I teased my tongue along my hand, took the shot slowly, savoring every moment, never once taking my eyes off Josie. Then I put the lime in my mouth and worked it like I was sucking a nipple.

"Damn," said Jordan. "You learn quick."

"It makes me wish I was a lime," said Josie with a wicked grin.

"Or a pile of salt," Jordan said.

The tequila was starting to hit me, and I was feeling bitchy and a little drunk. Reaching for the salt shaker, I grabbed Josie's hand and pulled it, palm up, toward me.

"Well, since you mentioned it…"

I licked her wrist slowly, sensually, then poured five times more salt than I needed for a tequila shot. I began to lick it off, taking more time than necessary, nibbling and kissing Josie's wrist, leaving red lipstick marks all over and looking up at her as I did. She watched me, enraptured.

I reached for the tequila shot, but Jordan was already holding it out for me with a smirk on her face.

I put the lime in Josie's hand, downed the tequila shot, pursed my lips, and pointed them at her.

Josie put the lime close to my mouth, making me move forward to get it. I bit into it, sucked, and she kept holding it, her fingers grazing my lips. I worked it more than I had before, opening my mouth to take Josie's finger and lick it as lime juice ran down her hand.

I looked into her eyes and noticed how cute she was, the same way I'd noticed when I first looked at her. She had big brown eyes and close-cropped black hair with Brylcreem or something on it, and a tattoo of a bat between her breasts, visible through the tank top. She was definitely a looker.

"Now you *have* to dance with me, Monique," Josie said. "Please?"

That had been my fourth shot, and I was feeling more than a little drunk. "You don't mind, do you, Jordan? Don't wait up."

"Oh, I won't," she smirked, and Josie led me out to the dance floor. Feeling drunk, I turned back and stuck my tongue out at Jordan, who responded by flipping me off. I tried to mouth "you wish" to her, but I was too drunk to form the words.

✠ ✠ ✠

By the time Josie and I started dancing, I was feeling drunk more from fear and excitement than from the tequila. I felt incredibly turned on, and I was doing something I never thought I'd be able to do: dance in public. I started to work my hips to the throbbing beat of Prodigy, just as Jordan had taught me. Josie started to dance too, making eye contact with me and not breaking it. I finally dropped my eyes, shutting them tight as I spread my legs and bent down low, pumping my hips suggestively.

"Where'd you learn to dance?" shouted Josie, loud enough that I could just barely hear her.

"Why?" I asked.

"You dance kind of like Jordan."

"We took the same dance class back in high school," I shouted back.

"You've known her that long?"

I nodded, lying through my teeth but not caring. I didn't want this woman to think I was Eliza Doolittle to Jordan's Henry Higgins, even if that's what I was. To take her mind off it, I turned up the heat, dancing closer and throwing every sexy trick Jordan had shown me. Josie matched my movements, our bodies brushing together periodically. Within a few minutes I was sheened with sweat, my breasts evident under the damp material of the white baby tee I wore—and I didn't care.

I slid my hand down my belly and spread it across my crotch suggestively, letting my other hand laze across my breasts, rubbing my nipples. Josie stared. I felt more like a stripper than a club girl, but I didn't give a shit any more. I had started out by hating her, but I was beginning to like Josie—or, at least like her attention. I'm not the kind of girl people look at, men or women. I just don't attract that kind of attention. This was the first time I felt like I was really getting it, and I had to admit it was turning me on.

After three songs, I didn't want to stop. Josie asked if I did, and I shook my head and we continued for three more. By then I was absolutely soaked, my baby tee practically see-through. I started wishing I'd worn a bra, even though I almost never wear one. Josie was soaked too; her tank top looked as if someone had dumped water on it. She had really nice breasts. I found myself wondering what they would feel like against me.

I got a little scared then. "I think I need a drink," I shouted.

"Let me buy," she said. "After that kind of a show I owe you something."

I would have blushed if I weren't already bright red from the heat. I went over to where Jordan had been sitting, but of course she was gone. I scanned the bar and the dance floor and didn't see her. I felt a stab of jealousy, wondering if she'd gone home already with some beautiful woman.

Josie waved to the bartender and ordered two tequila shots.

"We're out of salt," the bartender said.

I didn't know what I was going to do until I found myself leaning hard against Josie, feeling her nipples and nipple rings hard against my flesh, and I was licking and sucking at her neck.

"Who needs salt?" I asked, and did the shot.

Then I kissed her on the lips, the taste of tequila mingling with the taste of Josie's mouth, and she kissed me back, putting her arms around me.

"Your turn."

"I don't drink," said Josie. "Go ahead."

I remember thinking that if I had another drink, I was going to do something I shouldn't, but then I was licking Josie's neck and ear, tasting her salt, licking my way up to her forehead and kissing and sucking it, and I remembered that that was the whole point—I was *supposed* to do something I shouldn't. I chased her salty sweat with the tequila and kissed her again, and I felt her dancing to the music, grinding her hips against mine, one of her knees thrust between mine, the tight leather pants riding up against my pussy, and I remembered how I hadn't worn anything underneath at Jordan's insistence: You get panty lines in leather pants that tight. Josie propped her foot up on the bar stool so that her knee pressed through the leather pants and against my bare pussy. I moaned into her hair and felt her hands sliding up my back under my crop top, caressing my sweaty flesh. I almost wasn't surprised when I felt one hand move around, still under the shirt, to touch my breast.

"Want to go somewhere?" I asked.

"What's wrong with right here?" she pinched my nipple until I squirmed. She rocked her knee against my crotch as we danced in time with the music.

"Get a room!" someone shouted, and I turned my head to see Jordan next to me, a pretty red-haired boy dyke in tow. "Need a ride somewhere, you two?"

I looked at Josie, who smirked.

"It's OK," she said. "I'll take her home."

✠ ✠ ✠

We hadn't been parked in front of my place for five seconds before she had her hands down my pants. She lowered the emergency brake and leaned across it, deftly undoing my button-fly leather pants. Feeling drunk and sexy, I just leaned back and threw my arms up over my head, arching my back so she could pull my pants down a little bit and get her hand in there—not very easy with them that tight.

All of a sudden I remembered that I wasn't wearing anything underneath them, and I imagined Josie unbelievably titillated by that fact as she touched my pussy, as she kissed me hard, her tongue working its way into my mouth while she found me wet and then let one finger, then two, slide into me, bringing moans from my lips. I put my arms around her neck and bucked my ass up higher, inspiring her to pull my leather pants down all the way to the tops of boots. I let my now-naked ass rest on the car seat as Josie pulled up my shirt and hungrily kissed my nipples. Then she was fingering me, teasing my clit with her thumb as she pumped three fingers into my pussy, so many it felt tight, so tight it almost hurt—but not quite. I still don't know how she got those skintight pants off over my boots, but my mind was clearly on other things. When I realized she'd taken them off, I felt a sudden wave of fear and realization at what I was doing, understood in a rush that I'd gone as far with a stranger as I ever thought I would, and decided I didn't want to stop now, not by a long shot. I was naked except for those high boots and the baby tee pulled up over my tits, so I didn't see any reason to wait until we could get into the house—even assuming Jordan hadn't taken her girl there.

And for the first time since the first night Jordan didn't come home, I didn't care. I lifted my naked ass off the seat, reached down to hit the lever that reclined it, and came down with a whoosh, lifting my boots onto the dashboard as I settled back down into the seat, scooting back as Josie climbed on top of me.

Josie was a smallish woman, a little shorter even than me, but I was still surprised that she managed to curl into that tiny space and get her mouth between my legs. I gasped as I felt her tongue on my clit; I moaned when I felt her two fingers go back inside me, felt her licking me so fast I almost couldn't stand it. It was almost too much, too much too fast. I was about to tell her to stop when something broke inside me, and the building numbness and discomfort gave way to a flood of pleasure and surrender. Josie's tongue on my clit suddenly felt like the most divine thing on the planet, better even—in that instant—than Jordan's.

I hadn't come from being eaten out in years, but I was getting there quick, my lessened inhibitions and intense arousal combining to bring me off quickly. But from the way I was moaning, Josie could tell how close I was, and she didn't want to relinquish me yet. I felt her fingers slip out of me, felt one hand moving up to gently squeeze my breast and pinch my nipple, felt her tongue swirling around my pussy lips and then into my entrance, felt her licking down lower. Jesus, no one but Jordan had ever done *that* to me before, but God, it felt incredible.

I pushed my booted feet on the dashboard and lifted my ass off the seat as her tongue slid between my cheeks and teased my asshole, licking harder as she discovered she hadn't offended me or turned me off. I felt the very tip of her tongue penetrating me as she worked her clit with her free hand. Then, willing or not, she made me come, and I didn't even have time to say it before it was happening. My climax exploded through my body, and I whimpered in pleasure as I sank back down onto the car seat.

"Fuck," I said. "You almost made me come just from going down on me."

"Was it good?" Josie asked.

"Fuck," I sighed. "It was incredible."

Josie slid her body up on top of mine, kissing me. I could taste myself, could smell my body on hers and hers on me.

"So, then…your name's Violet?"

I stopped, my heart suddenly pounding, like I'd been caught in an evil lie.

"Why do you ask?"

"Well, this is Jordan's house," said Josie. "I gave Jordan a ride home a few times. I know she lives with her lover, Violet. Or at least, she did. Are you a new roommate or something?"

"No," I said sadly. "I'm Violet. I'm sorry Jordan lied to you."

"Why?"

"Why am I sorry or why did she tell you my name is Monique?"

"Both."

I shrugged. "She thought you wouldn't want to sleep with me if you knew I was her girlfriend."

"Fuck that! Jordan has great taste in women. I guess I would have thought it was weird that she was pimping you, but I probably would have been fine with it."

"She was not pimping me!"

"Anything you say," smiled Josie. "You're beautiful."

"Are you fine with it now?" I asked her.

"More than fine with it," Josie said. "I think we should go inside."

"Fuck," I said. I pulled my T-shirt down and looked around

on the street. "I don't see Jordan's car. I don't know if she's coming home. She could be here any minute."

"Why should that make any difference?"

"Maybe even with that girl she picked up."

"So I ask again, why should that make any difference?"

"It's a one-bedroom."

"Uh-huh."

"With only one bed."

Josie chuckled and raised her eyebrows. "Sounds good to me," she said.

"Oh, my God," I said. "You're serious."

Josie just winked and kissed me.

I thought about it, thought about my Pygmalion being there to see her Galatea make it with this handsome dyke on the bed we shared. God, there would be so many hours of processing after this one I couldn't even begin to count them. I looked at Josie and smiled.

"Hand me my pants," I said.

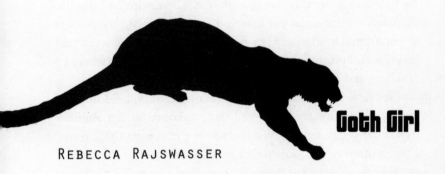

Goth Girl

Rebecca Rajswasser

It was a late-summer night. A new city, a new moon. She—my girlfriend, my partner, my mistress, led me down cobblestone streets flooded with human specimens ripe for our eyes to pick from. We rounded a dark corner and slipped into the club door, marked only with a red V for "Vortex"—or at least that's what it said on the flier a lanky androgyne had handed us on the street a few minutes before. On our side of the chain-link fence, a beefy bouncer checked our IDs and stamped our hands.

The space inside was thick with smoke. A small army of young men and women in black and burgundy, velvet and lace swayed through the gray air of this dance hall tomb. Bright laser lights spun around the room, revealing tight pockets of the "goth girls" my girlfriend talked about so often. They danced to their own macabre beat, stretching their platform-clad feet out from under long black dresses as their pale white hands with vampire nails danced in front of their downcast faces. They moved languidly through the smoky soup. Their ebony hair barely had the strength to bend or sway. Their eyes, trained so well by their ecstasy trances, watched the floor silently from behind white powder and black paint.

She pulled me to the center of the concrete dance floor, and we danced together. It was strange being here with her, outside the safety of our usual gay bars and fetish clubs. But I was soon so enraptured by the way her body moved to this wayward beat that the background faded and we could have been anywhere or nowhere and I wouldn't have noticed or cared.

Her new black Dickies hung low on her hips, held in place by the black G.I. Jane belt—all that remained of her military days. I loved that belt. I loved the way she moved in those pants. I loved the way she looked that night, from head to toe. I loved the way the fluorescent light of the dance floor caught the blond fuzz on her head, flashing little sparks. I loved the way she had shortened her pendant so that it hung right in that sexy nook between her clavicles. I loved the way her breasts hung under her skimpy white tank top, and I loved the line that tank top drew along her sides and down her middle, exposing her soft, just-round-enough belly.

The ragged edge created when she'd taken out her bowie knife and cut off the bottom of her tank top rolled up just a little as her hips rose and fell, as if issuing an invitation it had no right to offer. She closed her eyes and let her head roll and swing as her arms rose up from her sides, and I could see tiny beads of sweat collecting in the brown silk under her arms. She turned her back to me, exposing that sweet alcove just above her belt-line, where she knew my fingers liked to linger and my mouth liked to kiss.

She stretched her arms behind her back and touched her self there, laughing, before turning to face me with her wicked grin.

I'd never seen her this bare before, not outside our rooms. I was crazy about this new look and she knew it. She was making the best of it. Perhaps she also knew, as she shook and wiggled a few feet away from me, how much it turned me on to see her out enjoying herself for once in something other than her usual baggy, faded jeans and oversized retro shirts.

Perhaps she kept that distance between us as we danced to torture me, or perhaps she did it because she was enjoying watching me as much as I was enjoying watching her. I was dancing for her, swaying my hips to the snaky rhythms so that she could see my firm thighs, exposed under the Catholic school skirt she liked so much.

I tore my eyes from her hips, and for a moment she held my gaze. Her face was so sweet, with her melted-honey eyes. I moved toward her and lifted my left hand to brush my knuckles gently across the soft skin of her cheek.

"Don't touch me," she said, turning her face away. I stepped back, surprised by my own obedience, and lowered my head. I clasped my arms behind my back to let her know she was in complete control and that I understood her wishes. She placed her hands behind her own back and hugged herself there, as if to tell me that she was not going to be touching me either. It was clear that this was a night for watching.

When the music changed she left me there, without a word, and went to the bar. I knew better than to follow her, not even with my eyes—not without her permission. I turned my back so I wouldn't be tempted and drank in the spectacle behind me.

A boy was watching me. He smiled as I caught his eye, and I knew I was part of the spectacle too. I turned away, tried to forget him, and went back to the dance. I let the slow syncopation of this new music enter my body. It moved me in unfamiliar ways, and I liked it. I found myself wringing my arms behind my back, above my head. My wrists pushed themselves together as if the bracelets I wore were bindings placed there by her hands. As if she had left me tied up as literally as she had in my mind, or as if the music had the power to do it on its own.

The music changed again. I turned around. Something moving on the stage behind me had caught my eye. It was a goth girl I hadn't seen before. She must have just come in, because there was *no way* I would have missed her. She was captivating. Unlike the others, she wasn't covered from head to toe in funeral crepe. Somehow she managed to retain a tinge of life and lightness underneath her vampiric doom. Her black dress was short, sleeveless, and fitted. There were laces, begging to be undone, down the back. Beneath it, her legs appeared to be bare until just below her calves, where her firm skin met the stiff leather of her Doc Martens.

Her face was naturally pale, accented deliciously by her cropped black locks and the thick line of black around her eyes. She danced with a dramatic air that made her impossible to ignore. The theatricality of her movements was augmented by the expressions on her lovely, tastefully painted face. This was not the thrown-together look of some preteen gothic wanna-be but the deliberate work of an artist, an actress, a star—the carefully constructed costume of someone ready to be watched. She smiled at me when she saw me watching, inadvertently and involuntarily doing her bidding, and then she continued to dance.

Immediately, without missing a beat in the music, I let my eyes travel across the room to scan the bar. I knew my mistress would like this morsel and that she would be furious with me if I let her miss such a lovely specimen. When my eyes finally found her, she was leaning against the bar, clove cigarette in hand. I had nothing new to tell. Her eyes had already found this dancing black fairy. I glanced from one to the other, smiled, then returned to my solitary dance.

The music changed again and again, still we danced. Each

time I looked up to find my lover's eyes, I found them still fixed on the gothic princess, dancing her dark drama. At first I was jealous. Then I saw her look my way. I knew she was just checking up on me. *She's totally smitten*, I told myself. *She can't even keep her eyes off the princess long enough to scold me with them.* The thought of my mistress so powerless under the spell of this young one was amusing enough to relieve me of my envy.

I watched my lover watch her new pet, imagining I could feel her desire growing within my own body, its wetness gathering between my legs. My pulse began to throb in time with the music as I let my eyes travel from the powerful eyes I knew so well, to the dark eyes of the stranger who had us both under her spell.

Suddenly our dark fairy was joined by another. She pulled her new friend close and they gyrated together. I wondered if they were lovers, or if our little actress-angel had added this new dimension to her show for our benefit. A new warmth rose in my body as our little voyeuristic trio took on a fourth player. I felt the heat rising to my face as my eyes sought out the greedy grin I knew would be waiting on my lover's face.

This is too hot, I thought, smiling at her. *Here I am watching her watch these dark angels dancing, and as we watch them a fire builds in our loins. She knows that me watching her watch them is getting me as hot as it is getting her. We're together.*

I danced around a little more, then moved to a spot across the room where I could watch my lover from afar. *What's she thinking?* I wondered. *What will she expect of me when we get home?*

Her imagination was boundless, so I knew I could be in for any number of treats or tortures. Would she punish me for watching so greedily? Would she wax dramatic and want to take on roles? Would she dress me up like the dark goddess diva and have her way with me? Would she punish her for being a shameless flirt?

Our ocular orgy and my internal flights of fancy were arrested when a voice came over the PA system a few minutes later, telling us the party was over. The music stopped, the lights came on, and the magic spell was broken. I watched my lover's eyes follow the angel out of the club. She looked at both of us as she passed, and I knew she had enjoyed our watching as much as we had.

My mistress and I were quiet as we left the bar. She smiled, wrapped her arm around my shoulder, and pulled me close to her. We passed the angel again on our way around the corner. She smiled at us, reserving a coy little shrug of her damask shoulders for my partner, who looked at me with her greediest grin.

We walked back to the car in silence, both of us replaying the dance club scenes in our heads. The pressure she put on my shoulder as we walked told me my mistress was pleased with me. I was glad we had been able to share those moments. There would be fun and games that night, and I would be both pun-ished and rewarded.

My excitement grew again as we dropped into her car. She popped a cassette into the player and drove home, eyes on the road with a wicked smirk pasted firmly across her lips. We rode in silence. I began to wonder if I had angered or disappointed her in some way. She wasn't usually this quiet. When she turned the car into her drive, I knew I could put that fear to rest.

She stepped out of the car, came around to open my door, and offered me her hand to help me out of the car. *Hmm. Chivalrous tonight,* I thought, though I didn't dare to be the one to break the silence. Once inside, I followed her straight to the spare room at the back of the house—the "playroom." She pointed to a spot in the middle of the hardwood floor, and I knew I was to stand and wait. She turned her back to me and opened the mahogany doors of her grandmother's armoire. I could tell she had something particular in mind, because she was taking her time, digging through the far corners of the closet.

Aha! I was right on the money! I said to myself as she pulled out a long, slinky black dress with flowing sleeves. I started to unbutton my coat as she reached into the closet for the fuck-me pumps she'd commandeered from my closet. The ones with the sculpted steel heels and the chain-link ankle straps. Then she stood up. I expected her to turn to me, order me to strip, then hand me her bounty of items, one by one. But she didn't. In fact, she barely even looked at me as she draped the costume over her arm and walked right out of the room.

"Don't even think about moving," she bellowed on her way down the hall.

I couldn't imagine what she was up to until finally I heard the telltale click of metal heels coming down the hallway. *Oh, my good goddess,* I thought. *She's put the outfit on herself!* I couldn't believe it. She wasn't going to let me be the diva after all; she was taking that choice role for herself.

She entered the room with an expectant glare in her honey eyes. "I saw that smile on your face while you were watching. I felt you boring into my brain to see what I was thinking. Let's see how close you came, let's see how well you know my desires." Then she walked to the CD player, pushed play, and started to dance. For a while I just stood there watching her move—the sway of her hips, her hands feathering before her, mocking that ecstasy trance.

I let my coat fall to the floor and sauntered over to her. I danced around her, taking her in. The curves of her body, which she so skillfully hid under her day-to-day boy drag, were elegantly exposed by the clingy black crepe. Her femininity was a surprise to my eyes and an enticing shock to my system. I slid my hands around her narrow waist and pulled her close to me. It was a delight to feel the soft roundness of her ass yield to my touch under the smooth fabric of the dress. "Mmm," I moaned in her ear as I ran my hands up and down her back, over her ass, down the sides of her thighs.

"Open my belt," I instructed as I continued to explore the effects of new wrapping on a familiar package. She did, then I pulled the open belt off my waist with a snap and brought it around behind her, catching her wrists on the way. I bound her arms behind her and led her to the wooden post at end of the leather bound bed. Pulling the belt tight, I tied her to the post, like a witch about to be burned at the stake.

Tracing the line of the leather cord around her neck, I reached into her dress and pulled her knife from its sheath. I shot her an evil grin as I tested the blade against my own finger before placing it, flat, against her neck. I ran the blade slowly across her clavicles, the exposed parts of her chest. I stuck its tip into the metal ring that held the zipper and pulled. I stepped forward and kissed her deeply while I ran the knife down her center, placed its cool blade flat into her nipples and pushed, hard.

"Open your mouth. Hold this," I commanded as I placed the blade between her teeth. Reaching behind her to free her arms, I took her breast in my mouth and caught her perfect nipple between my teeth. I let my tongue play there for a minute before releasing her and letting the belt flop down on the bed. The dress fell from her shoulders and crumbled to the floor. She looked beautiful standing there, and I suddenly wanted to see her in softer light. Pulling the lighter I carried only to light her cigarettes out of my pocket, I lit the three large, black candles that stood in wrought-iron holders on either side of the bed.

I placed my hand around the back of her neck and pulled her closer. "Arms up," I ordered, still amazed that she would listen. I took the knife from her mouth then turned her around so her back was to me. We moved away from the pole to stand in front of the bottom of the bed. I slipped her wrists into the restraints that hung from the bedposts. I ran my hands, then my nails, over her smooth, muscular back, leaving tiny red traces like map lines in her flesh. Reaching one hand around in front of her, cupping her breasts, I pulled her hips back to give me full access to her perfect ass. I ran my free hand over each perfect mound, squeezing and caressing that delicate meat. Then, mustering all the courage I could, I drew back my arm and let it land with a loud smack. I felt her body contract in my arms as I let one slap then another come down on her smooth skin. Again and again my open palm met her slowly reddening ass.

She took it well and proudly, as I knew she would, barely letting out the quietest moan. I could see her face in the mirror at the other end of the bed. Her cheeks were red and her eyes clamped shut. I could tell she was struggling with her pride.

I pushed her forward and away from me as I turned to the armoire to select a whip. I chose the first cat she had ever used on me, the one with the thick suede strands. Running the soft strands across her skin so she'd know what was coming, I bit into her neck, her earlobe, then whispered in her ear, "It was very nasty of you to flirt with my girlfriend on the dance floor. You know that, don't you?"

"Mm-hmm," she answered.

"Excuse me?" I asked, startling even myself.

"Uh, yes, yes, it was very nasty of me."

"And are you sorry?"

"Yes, yes, I'm sorry," she stammered.

"Not sorry enough," I answered, stepping back from her and letting the whip fall against her back. She grunted in spite of herself as I took the stance I'd seen her take so many times and let the whip fall again across her shoulders. I swung the whip around, hitting one shoulder, then the other, hitting her ass, her hips, the backs of her thighs. She was not good at standing still, but I didn't mind. I liked to watch her body snake and curve, so sexy, so feminine. Her soft moans and grunts turned into delicate cries and whimpers. I focused my swing to one spot on her shoulder.

I let the whip fall softly at first, enjoying the sound of the suede on her flesh. As her skin turned rosy in the candlelight I let the blows fall harder and harder until the pink turned to purple, her reserve fell away and she let loose a cry, then a scream. I dropped the whip to my side and slid between her and the bed, taking her in my arms and kissing her gently.

"Yes, yes my dark angel, it's OK," I cooed, running my hands over the hot welts on her back. I held her while she caught her breath, then reached up and released her wrists from the cuffs.

She pulled me to her and buried her face in my neck. I held her while she cried, wondering how long she had wanted to play out this fantasy, how long she had wanted to be on the other end of the whip's bite. I reached down to where her dress had fallen and draped it around her shoulders. "It's OK, baby, it's OK, I whispered as we walked out of the room and down the hall.

I turned down the satin sheets and helped her into bed. Leaving my clothes in a heap, I crawled in beside her and held her while the light of a new day came through the open window. This had truly been a night to remember. A spontaneous release that began at the Vortex, a place we had fallen into purely by chance.

Rebecca Rajswasser

Peaches and Orchids

DeLaine

"I'm tired of this shit!" she hissed at me through the blaring music and the noise of the crowd.

"Yeah? So am I!"

"Then why don't you get out of this? I'm going home!"

As she walked away I felt as though a huge weight had been lifted. Things had gotten so bad all of a sudden, and neither of us knew how to make them better. There was no doubt in my mind that I loved her. We had been together for two years—of course I loved her. Why else would I still be with her? Right?

My best friend, Cass, spotted me immediately through the crowd of sweaty, dancing lesbians. "Where's Deidre?" she asked as she sipped her Hennesey and orange juice. Cass is a truly a ghetto superstar and the best friend a person can have. Though she's loud, obnoxious, and not at all prone to holding her tongue, she speaks the truth. I knew Cass would be offended by Deidre's sudden disappearing act, but hell, so was I.

"She left," I replied nonchalantly.

"Why?"

"She got pissed off at me. She says I don't treat her like a girl-friend."

"You don't," Cass said, draining her cognac. "Well, she could have said goodbye to me. Shit, I didn't do anything. Oh, well, fuck it! Let's go dance with the pretty ladies!"

"Cool."

As we walked to the dance floor I felt a pang of guilt, as though I was doing something wrong by continuing to party after my girlfriend had just walked out. A part of me wanted to run after her and make things better. But I had done that too many times, and besides, Cass would've cussed me out. So my guilt and I stayed at the club.

The music was throbbing. Hot female bodies bounced all around. Tits and ass nudged me playfully as I headed to the dance floor, beer in hand.

"Hi," she said.

"How you doin'?" I replied.

"Have I met you before?"

We both knew this was our first meeting. Hell, I would remember a face and body like hers, but I decided to play along.

"Maybe," I said. "What's your name?"

She came close to me and slid her arm through mine. I felt the heat of her breath and moisture of her lips on my ears.

"NaLing," she purred.

"Hi, NaLing. I'm DeLaine."

"Nice to meet you again, or for the first time, DeLaine." She was playing with me. "Why'd she leave?"

"Who?" I inquired, completely oblivious to the fact that Deidre had left me moments ago.

"Your girlfriend. That was your girlfriend who just left you here, right? I saw you guys arguing."

"Oh, yeah, my girlfriend. She got pissed off at me and decided to go home."

NaLing took my hand and planted a sensuously wet kiss on my palm of my hand. "She made a big mistake."

I tried to smile and break the trance this woman was putting me under, but it was useless, and I honestly didn't want to fight it. It had been two years or more since I had been flirted with, and never had such a beautiful Asian woman come on to me. I had always believed Asian women were some of the sexiest women on the planet, but I never thought I'd meet one who'd be interested in me! NaLing was about 5 foot 5, a couple of inches shorter than me, and had the most amazing long jet-black hair. Her dazzling green eyes were exquisitely shaped. She wore a short black dress with no hose, sandals, and red polish on her toenails and fingernails. Her small frame slithered seductively next to mine as we made our way to the center of the dance floor.

There was no space between us when she slid her arms around my neck, then asked, "Is it all right to do this?" She didn't need to ask.

"Why wouldn't it be?" I replied, feeling like I was on my way to heaven and enjoying every second of the trip.

She coquettishly held my chin and said, "Baby, you have a girlfriend. I don't want to cause any problems."

"We've had problems before. Don't worry about her. Right now, worry about me."

I had never been so bold! I was shocked! It felt so good to be touched by someone new and beautiful. The music continued to thump while NaLing performed for me and on me. She twisted and turned, ground and grated her pelvis deep into my thigh. We were connected on the floor in a ceremony of dry humping, bumping, and gyrating in the murky red light of the club.

Cass knocked me from my trance. "Girl! What are you doing?" she asked.

"What does it look like I'm doing? This is NaLing, NaLing, this is my best friend, Cass."

"NaLing, mmm, what a wonderful name—but it sounds like trouble to me."

"Cassy, get lost," I said lightheartedly.

"See, I told you it was trouble," Cass said. "You're already sending your best friend of 15 years away. But anyway, I won't tell. You lovebirds have fun." With that Cass spun around and disappeared into the crowd.

"Sorry about that," I said. "She's just trying to warn me to be careful."

"I'm the one who should be careful of you," NaLing said as she rested her back against my chest and held my hands.

"Why?" I teased. "I'm completely harmless. Plus, I've got a girlfriend."

"Don't remind me. Let's just dance."

Her body was so limber and strong. Our eyes locked as I drove my knee between her legs. I could feel myself inside her. The beat of the music was flowing through us.

NaLing let her spaghetti strap fall down, and I began to kiss the curve of her shoulder. Her fragrance was that of peaches and orchids, and I was high on her. With the pounding of each beat, we clung together. We hadn't kissed; our lips only slid over and tickled each other's cheeks.

I could no longer hold back as NaLing moved her ass into my pelvis, ran her hands through her thick black hair, and began bucking up against me. My hands glided down her sides, finally resting on her hips. I pulled her into me and started thrusting. I wanted to fill her up, and I wished I'd worn my cock. She responded by tossing her head back, exposing her graceful, smooth neck, and letting out an incredible moan.

One of her hands dropped between her thighs, and the other pulled my face to her neck. I kissed and sucked while she continued to rub. There were so many people on the floor that no one seemed to notice what we were doing, and I didn't care if they did. I just wanted to taste her.

I spun NaLing around and picked her up as she wrapped her sexy legs around my waist, and then I banged her some more. She put her fingers in my mouth and let me taste and smell the essence of her womanhood, peaches. I felt drugged. I was trippin' like I can't remember trippin' before. I carried her to the wall and pinned her hands as we finally kissed. She moaned and bucked as though she was going to come from our kiss alone. I slid my hands inside. Hot wetness smothered my fingers, and I felt her throb. I tickled and pinched her until I saw her eyes roll back as she bit her lip and collapsed in my arms.

I gave NaLing a kiss on the forehead and asked her if she wanted a drink. She declined. She then thanked me for a wonderful dance and started to walk away. I wanted to ask for her number, but I knew I just couldn't deal with any more stress at the time—I still had to go home and deal with Deidre.

As I looked on, she stopped at this very butch girl who nodded to me, then kissed NaLing roughly on the mouth. The two grabbed hands and exited the club.

STRIP JOINTS

Temptations

LOUISE KINGTON

It was that old line—"What's a girl like you doing in a place like this?"—except in this case "girl like you" referred to me, one voluptuous 20-year-old dyke, and the "place like this" was a grungy strip club, deep in the bowels of the seediest part of town. As I scanned the dimly lit tables filled with old men and the occasional boy full of drunken bravado, I asked myself the same question I'd asked Michelle: *Lesbians in lap-dance establishments?* Michelle's answer was simple: "I really think I have a chance with these girls. Think about it."

Michelle and I worked together as menial checkout chicks. I hadn't known about her, and she hadn't known about me. I don't think anyone is looking to find like-minded people working at their local supermarket! But then one night I spotted her at my favorite gay bar, and after a few "Oh, my Gods" and "You're gay too?" we became friends.

Now, looking around at the strippers that night, I hardly thought it was likely we'd have a chance with them (or even want one). Their teased hair, fake breasts, and overblown make-up didn't scream "dyke" to me. And the attention we were getting was just too much. We'd been let into this place for free, while all the guys had lined up to pay $10.

It was obvious our presence excited the men, which led them to spend more money. When Michelle and I had each gotten a lap dance, they got even more excited and spent even more money, and soon the sleazy guy at the entrance had a shit-eating grin from ear to ear. We were a sound investment!

It hadn't taken me long to figure out the rules here. The girls came on in sets of four. They danced on the stage and then stripped. They teased the men with their naked bodies and waited. Sooner or later the men would wave grubby $5 and $10 bills in the air. You could touch them, rub their breasts, and talk with them, but at all times the girls kept one hand over their cunt. They didn't want a riot! For $35 the girl of your choice would take you to a corner and give you the deluxe version.

After an hour of this I was bored. Michelle, however, was having a grand time. She had found some 30-year-old guy who was offering her a night with his wife, who was stripping for the first time. I don't remember her stage name, but it was probably Ambrosia or Eden or Tia. The girl in question was, I guess, conventionally good-looking. But I doubted she'd know how to play with a pair of breasts! At least this loser guy was buying Michelle drinks. I sucked on my beer and slumped in my seat, intent on drinking myself into oblivion.

Oblivion never came. Somewhere between pissed and smashed I sat up *in a hurry*. Strutting down the stage, with a devil-may-care attitude, was definitely a dyke. I could feel my pulse start to race. Her short hair, shaved at the back, stocky build, and tattoos clashed with red lipstick on the biggest pair of lips I'd seen in a long while. She was the lay of my dreams! Gina Gershon in *Bound* had nothing on this dyke! In a leather bra, breasts spilling over the top, and matching tight leather hot pants laced up the side and slung low on the hips, she was irresistible. And she could *move*. Her hips gyrated urgently, suggesting an intimacy I could only dream about. Her hands slid expertly over her body, stopping only to tweak a nipple or lightly touch herself as she bent over. She left the insipid waifs with their '80s hair for dead.

I suddenly had the desire to part with a $5 note. Nudging Michelle to pay attention, I waved my money. The desirable dyke sauntered over after her song ended. She reached for my money, and then with a whispered "spread 'em, darlin'," she proceeded to move over me like nothing else. My hands were on her breasts, her stomach, her thighs; part of me cringed at just how low I had sunk in my desire for sexual gratification, but only *part* of me!

"It's so good not to feel a dick nearly up my ass," she whispered. I blinked in surprise, not sure she had really made such a statement. The loud, thumping dance music matched my heartbeat. I looked around. Had anyone else heard? Men of all ages and sizes returned my gaze. Some looked away quickly or stared intently at their beers when they were caught watching. Others continued to stare at *my* hands on *her* breasts, *her* stomach, and *her* thighs. I was pleased with their attention.

All I could muster was a drunken and very lame "I think you're sexy." She laughed as she walked away, acknowledging my comment with a wink.

My mind had melted, but my mission was clear. While Michelle worked out the finer details of her little threesome, I would drink my way through the sets of girls until it was the dyke's turn again. And then I would shell out another five bucks.

By now I was convinced she was gay. My desire for her body would not allow any other ending to my story but us in bed fucking madly. When she came for her $5 I would ask her back to my place. Simple as that, I thought with drunken confidence.

The songs pounded on, the girls came and went, and the crowd steadily dwindled as dawn approached. Then she appeared. I fumbled in my haste to find my sweaty money and had to endure watching her perform a $10 job for a middle-aged man. I felt a surge of jealousy. I didn't want to share her body with anyone else. Her wink in my direction halfway through her dance calmed me.

She came over, fell to her knees, and with her teeth took the money from me. Her mouth was so close to my cunt it started to burn. I visualized us naked together. As she started to glide over my body I took a deep breath and leaned in. In my mind, her bra and leather pants had been discarded, and I imagined my mouth on her firm juicy breasts. Even her smell was arousing. A thin layer of glistening sweat formed on her body as she danced, and I wanted to taste it. To taste her. Everywhere. Her eyes were closed, her red lips slightly parted, and she started to breathe heavily as she gave the performance her all. Her breath on my skin was like a jolt of electricity. It was intense to the point of a delicious agony. It seemed like an eternity had passed before I realized our time together was ending and it was my last chance for action.

"Would you like to come back to my place?" I asked.

She froze and stood up. I didn't know what to do. As she looked at me with those big brown eyes I mumbled, "Forget it…I was only kidding," and let out a nervous laugh. And then, without a second glance, she walked away.

Inside I was dying. Images of us together naked with me kissing her gorgeous breasts faded into a nightmare of lonely masturbation. I suddenly felt very ill. Too much beer and rejection to boot. I looked around desperately for Michelle. I wanted to go home. Apparently not wanting to interrupt my lap dance, Michelle had quietly left to meet with the guy and his stripper wife.

I slowly stood up, the room spinning slightly, and aimed toward the exit of the club. I was nearly there when I noticed her again. She was walking directly toward me. With a slight smile she brushed past, handing me something as went by. I turned only to see her spiderweb–tattooed behind disappear. With trembling fingers I opened the note. Five words scrawled across the page: "Meet me at the bar."

Caramelle Kisses

JIANDA JOHNSON

Caramelle whispered softly as she sat on my lap, stroking my short 'fro like a handful of trim. The girl was so drunk. She could be Rachel True's stand-in—you know, that beautiful black girl in the film *The Craft*—10 years down the line. She was just as bewitching.

"I'm not from here," she said, smiling. She shifted her body, and her low-cut, shimmering gray blouse revealed a hint of her left tit. I kept swinging my head around, thinking the big old bouncer was going to kick my dykey ass, but he just looked on, drooling, as did the men in the seats behind our table.

"Do I make you horny, baby?" she asked.

We chuckled together as she recited the droll *Austin Powers* line. I love sexy women with a sense of humor. It was a shame she was so shit-faced. I had wanted to ask her out for drinks after the show.

See, I was drooling too but didn't know it. It was my first trip to Vegas, my first lap dance, my first strip club, and my first lesbian come-on. *I* usually did all of the coming on.

Usually too I'm the "look but don't touch type," yet there I was in Club Paradise with a lap full of Caramelle, just creaming. She was a slim girl—not usually my type, since I love meat. But her performance was meaty, that's for damn sure. A few moments before, homegirl was on stage in a skintight black leather catsuit, strutting in time to Madonna's "Burnin' Up." Watching her take that thing off had made me want to genuflect.

Mother Mary help me if that girl didn't peel it off, stripping down to a G-string, her peach of a pussy shaved down to the nub, looking straight at me like this was her *soul* she was baring, just for me. My eyes probed her. I wanted it. Had to have it. Couldn't touch it! At least I thought so until she ran backstage, changed, and came around to our table—the only table of women in the club. She was either seriously turned on by so much attention from a group of dykes or she was an incredible actress.

"Buy me a drink?" she had asked, staggering up to my friend Kelly.

Kelly, a lean, athletic soft butch, had averted her eyes from Caramelle to her girl, Felicia, sitting to her left. Caramelle, unfazed by Kelly's silence, swirled her fingers inside Kelly's purse and, as if she were a magical fairy, beckoned the money to flow forth. It worked.

Felicia, ultrafemme and always overprotective of Kelly, ordered the drink. "I'll handle this," she said to our lanky, somewhat aroused waiter, then ordered Wyder's Ciders all around. Caramelle insisted on a Zima.

"Uh, um, no problem, ladies!" the waiter had said. When our hapless servant brought our drinks a few minutes later, he zeroed in on Caramelle's generously large breasts. A beige areola and half of her suckable, rock-hard nipple were peeking out from the side of her blouse. We all knew it, and so did she. I licked my lips, thirsty for a little something *extra*.

The waiter brushed up against Caramelle and set a Zima down at our table—such a femme's drink! We eyed her hungrily as she took the bottle between her hands, rubbing it up and down. Stripper's foreplay. Her lips circled around it as she eyed me, dead on.

I shifted in my seat. My cunt was hot for her, and she must have sensed it. She plopped right down in my lap, and that's when she started in with the "I'm not from here" business. Prince's "Sexy Motherfucker" blared from the loudspeaker. Caramelle dropped her drink and dropped to her knees. My crew laughed in amazement, then gawked, hot and shameless. Being a virgin to such seduction, all I could really do was lie back and enjoy it.

Caramelle spread my legs apart and worked her hand up the inside of my black skirt.

"Yes, honey!" Kelly whooped, then quickly retreated as Felicia glared, jealous and horny for more at the same time.

My own hot drama played on as Caramelle pulled my skirt up until my panties were showing. The AC in the club blaring, my exposed flesh playing peekaboo, all eyes on us—my pussy reacted, twitching. Baby girl was *working it*, sucking up the attention.

"Oh," I moaned, my whole body shivering as she rubbed her breasts against my clit. Caramelle leaned forward into me, her breasts heaving, as if it were my cue to nurse, suckle, nuzzle, imbibe. Would that I could, I'd have devoured her right there.

"Hold up!" a male voice bellowed. *Now* the bouncer reacts.

Caramelle quickly got up, turned around, and pressed her ass right into my lap, grinding and shaking her tits to the music.

Do you know how hard it is not to reach around and grab you by the nipples, sister? I thought. *To squeeze your heaving tits together and tell you whose these are?* I tried to send my lust by telepathy, gasping for air in my wanting her.

I pressed my thighs tightly together and moved in time with her rhythm. As my pussy lips rubbed up against each other, I edged up in my seat so that my breasts smashed up against her back when she got close.

It would be so quick—so easy—for you to place your hand over my clit. Just so easy. Consume me. Take me over.

The song ended. My private dancer got up and waved her tight butt back and forth in front of my face. Her creamy dark skin taunted me. I ached to be touched, to bed her, to feel the girl in my bed beside me, desiring my mouth on hers while my fingers worked inside her, fast and furious.

I wondered why I had to pop my lesbian cherry here in public with a bunch of my friends and all the men in the club gawking. I wanted to run away with my new lovergirl and consummate this lust in private.

Stevie Wonder's "Gotta Have You" began to play. Funkified, Caramelle pushed me back in the chair, climbed on top of me and kissed me hard and quick on the lips as she danced in time to this new, libidinous jam. Instinctively, I grabbed her hand and shoved it toward my pussy, but she backed away. She looked flustered, as if she needed guidance.

I couldn't take advantage, could I?

Together, we turned our heads toward the stage. A sexy, vinyl-clad blond dominatrix was straddling the floor, making humping motions. A brunet with humongous breasts strutted through the sequined stage curtain, slid underneath the blond, and spread her legs open. The blond snapped her fingers at the girl, lifting her head in complete confidence, smiling at the audience as if she had conquered us all.

Obedient, the brunet rolled over as the domme stroked her backside, then spanked it. She beamed while being disciplined, her plump bottom wiggling while we watched, transfixed.

How can they do this in public? I wondered. *It's not fair.*

"That's my friend," Caramelle whispered—loudly—toward me. "We fucked once."

"Which one?" Felicia yelled.

Hey, that's great. Uh, I need to use the restroom for a minute. Wait here for me? I wanted to ask. *I could say that,* I thought, *or I could curl my finger at her, sultrily gesturing at her as if to say, "Follow me."* How in the world did gay boys do this? They're so cool, so nonchalant, so horny. Me? Well, I only had the last part nailed.

Half hopeful, half delusional, I excused myself, glancing back two, maybe three times, hoping somehow my newfound sexy friend might take a cue.

When the song ended and I returned, I learned Caramelle had left for the night. No dancing, no "here's my number," nothing. She had probably passed out in some fortunate bouncer's backseat.

Kelly and her girlfriend drove me back to the Luxor, the posh hotel where we were staying Our beds were cozied right up against each other. I closed my eyes, and as my friends turned out the lights, I beamed myself into my own world. Their sheets rustled, and within minutes I heard their pussies grinding together, the sounds of their lovemaking evidenced by wet lips and fingers banging up against one another. My fingers made their way to my mound and found my hard little clit, craving a nice, rough fuck. As I listened to my friends making love, I shoved my middle finger inside myself, spread my legs far apart, and rode myself—hard.

"These girls can't dance," Caramelle had told me at the club. "I'm an artist. I put a dancer's touch into my sets. Did you like what you saw?"

"Mmm-hmm," I said now, arching my back.

Kelly and her girlfriend stopped dead silent, but for me it was too late. I couldn't stop. I pulled my bra down tightly under my breasts so they were thrusting upward, and moved a second finger deep inside myself, fucking in time to "Sexy Motherfucker" in my head, wanting to come so badly I couldn't stand it.

Kelly got up, I think. And I think I heard her girlfriend slap her lightly. I don't know. All I heard was my own desire as I swirled my fingers inside my pussy. Ovals became circles became ovals and circles…tighter, faster, round and round inside my wandering imagination.

I thought of Caramelle—only Caramelle—teasing me for drinks, for money, for attention. I didn't care then, and I didn't care now.

I spread myself wide open, and got myself close to the point of coming.

"Turn over," a woman's voice said. I did.

A finger probed me and a good pain shot up through the base of my spine.

"Mmm," said another voice, lighter this time.

I felt a dildo inside my slippery wet pussy. My face pressed into the pillows. Caramelle. She came back to please me, for free…

"I'm your Caramelle tonight," Kelly whispered. "Mmm, hmm," Felicia agreed.

They giggled to each other, in deep, resonant lovers' tones. One hand grabbed the side of my ass cheek, and another slipped in and out of me, alternately stroking my gyrating clit, kneading and working my supple bottom like we'd done this many, many times before. Then a thumb found its way inside my pussy, and I shifted my hips up into it as I whispered, "Yes, more," and the dildo moved around to my ass.

More good pain. "More!" I begged, yelling now, as my body writhed in complete submission and I came. My pussy had never shivered so hard. Shocks and waves bathed my body in light, and I was forced to relent.

I had worked myself into a frenzy all night, and after coming, all I wanted to do was be very still. As long as I kept my eyes
closed, I could pretend. *Lap dancers need love too*, I could tell
myself. All I needed now was to nestle myself in Caramelle's
bosom and go to sleep.

I kept my eyes closed. I felt hands stroking my cunt, drunk
with desire, all over again. Then a tongue. A thumb.

"Let her rest, sweetheart."

"Hold me, Caramelle," I said, more than a little drunk in my
own right, my eyes still shut tight for dear life. "Just hold me."

I heard another giggle. I reached out my arms like a baby
craving succor and felt two round, warm silky breasts in my face.
I heard a bra unsnap. Felt my dream girl lying beside me. Tucked
my head inside the softness. Fell asleep in the clouds.

BATHHOUSES

Please Untie Me

SARAH B WISEMAN

The sauna begged for naked bodies to lay themselves down on its sweet scented cedar and sweat until dawn. My ex begged too when we happened upon each other there early in the night. My libido was thrilled by the prospects of the bathhouse, and fucking my ex seemed like a comforting way to ease my way into a night of easy women. She moaned lovingly when I held her down and wrapped her boy body around me. She obeyed sweetly when I told her to sit, spread, come. We fucked in familiar desire to new rhythms, rocking the cedar bench until we were satisfied, our kisses solid and final. We parted, armed with desires we had taken from each other, ready for new and assorted thighs.

I headed up to the dance floor, looking forward to tincturing some stranger's lips, but on my way I was drawn into watching four women fucking on the red velvet spanking bench in the upper hallway. They were a beautiful sight, and one that I would come back to again and again throughout the night.

Two women were sitting on the bench with their backs to the wall. Another woman was kneeling in front. They held and fondled her as she leaned into them. The fourth woman was kneeling behind the third, rubbing her back, her ass, her cunt, her clit. Tasting, teasing, and applying lube. Across the room I spotted a gorgeous goth femme, also engrossed in the spanking-bench spectacle. I watched her as she watched.

Finally, though, I drifted away in hopes of becoming my own spectacle elsewhere. I had been on a high ever since I'd stood in line outside the house, waiting to get inside. It was my first visit to a bathhouse, and I was extremely nervous, which seemed to add to my high. As I stood in line, I'd looked around at the women waiting with me and laughed at the idea that in an hour or two I could be rolling around with one of them. I had tried not to work up my expectations. Just being at the bathhouse to watch would be enough, I had told myself. But now that my body was slick from sex with my ex, I felt like I had to move on to other women. I expected to find a shy butch to play with.

I wandered about the house listening to the sounds of pleasure-seeking, pleasure-giving, and pleasure-getting women, growing less nervous and more excited as I explored. After a while I made my way down to the sauna again. I couldn't resist its heat and scent.

Inside, two naked women were sweating in the dim red light. When I entered, one of them exited, and I realized I was left there with the goth femme I had seen watching the spanking-bench scene. I considered asking her what she had most liked about it, but before I had a chance, she moved close to me so our thighs were touching and asked if I wanted to kiss her. I immediately said yes to her thickly underlined eyes.

The scent of cedar mixed deliciously with the sensation of her dark, intriguing lips on mine. After a minute she said she needed to cool off in the showers, so we left the sauna together. I started to think about what, if anything, I might want with this gorgeous goth.

The shower room was empty, for the moment. Under separate showers we rinsed and writhed in the rush of cold water. Then she came up behind me, turned my shower off, and pushed me gently against the cold tile wall. I turned around, and we played lightly. The feeling of lips to lips held me there, but I quickly established that this was about as far as things would go for me. There was no continuous ripple in my cunt urging me to keep taking control. Nothing that made me want to push into her and not let go. I tried to think of ways I could turn her down politely—like "I don't have much to give tonight" or "You're not my type" or even "Sorry, baby, maybe next time."

As we kissed I felt her fingers touch the long black cloth I had wrapped around my waist. She pulled away from me and asked coyly, "What's this?" looking at the tie.

It's for tying up some pretty butch with that begging look in her eyes, I thought.

But what I said was, "Um, it's for tying…you know."

I wondered why I sounded, and felt, so shy. I knew I didn't want to tie her up. I tried to think of how to best turn her down again. But before I could muster up anything, she said, "Can I use it?"

"For what?" I immediately asked, taken off-guard. And then I thought, *She must think I'm an idiot. What else would it be for?* But she had this look in her eyes that I couldn't quite figure out.

"To tie you up," she answered.

I just stood there, staring at her black-lined lips, shocked. I didn't understand.

"If you don't want to, just say no; it's fine," she said.

And then it all came together. Her "don't fuck with me" goth femme–dominatrix aura suddenly shouted at me. She wanted to tie *me* up. I almost said "Oh, shit" out loud. I realized I'd have to tell her I didn't bottom. I tried to say something, but my shyness kicked in again and I could hardly speak. I couldn't even think. I just looked at her.

Eventually she kissed me deeply and said, "It's OK, don't worry about it," then started to walk away.

"I…I…" I stuttered. She turned back toward me with raised eyelids, and I suddenly heard myself say, "Yes," loudly, all the while thinking, *I should really take the easy way out.*

She smiled and said, "Yes, what?"

"I…" I stuttered again, wondering what I was doing. And then somewhere I found a voice, "I want you to tie me up, I just…I'm not usually the one tied…I mean, I usually do the tying…I mean, but I want to. Yes."

I was being flipped. And suddenly I wanted it badly. I wanted her badly. I wanted her to tie me up and fuck me hard, and I wanted to not be able to do one damn thing about it. I knew people got flipped all the time, but those people had never been me. This concession took a lot more guts than I usually had stashed with me at any given time—even, or maybe especially, with my longtime lovers. But just the thought of letting this goth femme domme me made blood flood to my clit in a rush. It was like I was taking hold of something I'd learned from someone else and unleashing desire's desire. And somehow it made me feel free.

"Well, since you said it so sweetly," she smiled, "I'd love to tie you up."

I leaned against the shower wall as she unwound the tie from my waist. "I like to do it this way," she said as she turned me around. She pushed me against the cold tiles so that she was behind me, pulled my wrists together behind my back, and tied them together.

"Tighter," I said, but I immediately thought, *What am I saying?* with a fleeting pang of fear.

She tied my wrists together tighter. The pang disappeared, and I felt safe. I felt wanted. She was so gentle. She pressed me against the wall, kissed my back, then my neck. She bent down and continued kissing all the way down. Her lips and tongue dragged down my back. I felt her short black nails scratch along my ass and felt her lips as she kissed my cheeks. Then she wrapped her hands around my thighs and, holding each one tight, spread my legs apart. I started to struggle against the tie in another brief wave of panic. But I stopped when I heard someone enter the showers. I knew someone was watching from behind, but I dared not turn around for fear my new lover would think I was distracted.

I struggled in lust this time to touch my ass to this goth femme's mouth. She wasn't going to let me have it that easily, though. Letting only her breath hit my ass, she pushed one finger through my lips into my cunt. I moaned and she withdrew. Her breath quickened as she squeezed between my legs and rotated so her back leaned against the shower tiles. Her one finger probed again, and her wet, wet mouth sucked on my clit, but just as quickly they were gone. *Oh, fuck,* I thought, yearning for more.

I felt her breath on my thighs now. I struggled to find her hand or her mouth again. Her mouth wrapped my clit but left again as soon as I moaned. One finger dove into me and then slid out. It was agony. I ached for more of her. Her hands held me away from crouching onto her. I struggled to no fucking end, my pussy swollen, wet, and tingling.

Finally, she led one finger inside me and held it there. She gave my clit another lick. I tried not to moan in case she'd withdraw. I wanted more mouth and more fingers inside me, but she was holding back. I felt another moist lick along my clit. I struggled and my knees weakened a bit. I heard women behind me talking about what was happening to me. I got more turned on by the voyeurs' voices as I struggled. Eventually I couldn't bear the ache anymore. I tried to say, "Put more fingers inside me," but it came out mostly as a moan, and she pulled the one finger that was there out.

"Ask nicely," she said, and licked me softly for a few seconds before pulling her mouth away again.

Asking at all was hard enough when I was used to demanding things. I struggled to make her do what I wanted, but I could barely bend or move since she was holding me so hard. I tried to convince myself that I could be polite.

"Will you put more fingers inside me?" I asked.

"That was a bit better," she said, and two fingers pushed against my cunt, pushing me open. It was more, but it wasn't enough. I clenched around her, the tingling in my pussy increasing.

"More," I managed to utter under quick breaths.

But she was determined. "What do you say?"

Oh, no, I thought. *Don't make me plead.*

Her lips went back to my clit, moving in slow circles for a second and then abruptly stopping. She put her thumb in my ass. I throbbed, quickly, sensations pulsing through me. I forgot myself in longing and released a loud, "Please!" My pride went down the drain as her fist pushed into me. I moaned and she didn't stop.

She fucked me and sucked my clit with hurried thrusts. I was already close to coming, and I wanted to see my voyeurs. In my struggle I pressed my tits harder against the cold shower wall. They shook against it in time with the thrusts in my cunt as my hips shuddered. As I started to come, my knees buckled and I tried to catch myself, but I quickly remembered that my hands were tied. I couldn't do anything but lean into the cold tiles and onto her. With a thrill I gave up struggling and let her fuck me, and I came over and over again until she decided I'd had enough.

Some time passed, and I was gently leaning against her. She asked if I wanted her to untie me. A small voice in my head told me I should really get out of this while I could. But I just whimpered softly, still blissfully lost, and uttered, "No." A cool shiver slipped down my spine.

A little later she asked again, "Do you want me to untie you?"

Again I said no, and before the small voice in my head could speak up, she swung me around and pushed me onto the floor. I struggled to get up but couldn't, since I was still tied. She turned the cold shower directly on me. I had a brief stroke of fear again, which quickly passed when she turned the shower off, flipped me onto my back, and stood above me, her legs apart, so I could see her slit and her clit swollen and sticky.

She bent so her lips hung closer and closer to my mouth. I tried to move my mouth up to her, to touch her, taste her, but I fell back onto the floor again, unable to maneuver. In that moment I remembered everything I love about giving women head.

Very nicely I said, "Could you untie me now, please?"

She moved her cunt nearer to me than before. Inches from me. My tongue raced toward it and my pulse sped up, but I couldn't quite reach it.

"I want you to beg," she said.

I don't beg, I thought, and then, *Aren't I already begging?* I looked at her like she must be kidding.

She stood up and walked her pussy away. She leaned against one of the walls and watched me lying there on the floor wanting her. She waited. She wasn't kidding. I could see her cunt lips from where I lay, and I wanted my mouth on them. I could see *she* wanted my mouth on them.

"Do you want to fuck me?" she asked.

I moaned, thinking, *Oh, fuck yes*, and then, *But I don't beg.*

"Do you want to fuck me, bitch?"

I moaned again at her insult. I relished in it, still a bit surprised at myself, despite where I was at that moment. I wanted more of her. I wanted to kiss her.

She stood staring at me. I looked at the people standing in the doorway watching. I looked at her and imagined her coming. That was enough to give me the strength to get up from where I lay. I crawled as best I could across the cool tile floor and brought myself to my knees in front of her. She put her foot on my shoulder. Her cunt glistened. My pride was already long gone.

"Beg, bitch," she said.

And I did. Graciously.

"Please untie me; I want your pussy," I said.

"How badly do you want it?"

"I really, really want it," I whined, and I tried to move my face in between her legs, but she held me back. She helped me stand up, then walked away toward the sauna, expecting me to follow. I did, finally able to fully see my audience. I was careful not to stumble as I squeezed between them through the sauna doorway. She held the door open for me and followed me inside. The deep red light and the heat swallowed me when I entered. I leaned my against one of the hot walls and watched her climb to the top cedar bench, sit, and spread her legs.

"Now what were you saying?" she asked.

"Please untie me," I said again. "I want to fuck you so badly." I walked up to her and knelt on the first bench so I could reach her. She put each of her legs over each of my shoulders and held me away from her. The smell of cedar mixing with her juices increased my craving.

"What do you want to do?" she pried, with a sly and impatient smile.

"I want to fuck you."

"What do you want?"

"I want to fuck you," I said. I was dying for her.

"So do it," she said, smoothly pushing her cunt into my face and between my lips. I swam deep, adoring the soft flesh in my mouth and under my tongue. But I felt restrained. I couldn't do everything I desperately wanted to do to her.

"Please untie me," I said. And then again, "Please. I want to use my hands. Please let me touch you. Let me fuck you with my hands. Please."

She moved her black nails down my back, letting one of her nipples slip into my mouth. I sucked, impatient and anxious.

"What do you want?" she asked.

"Please," I moaned, "please let me fuck you with my hands. Please!"

Her hands slowly unwound the tie around my wrists. *Finally.*

"Fuck me," she said, leaning against the wall. I moved my hands to her thighs resting on my shoulders and brought them down around my waist.

"Now," she demanded.

My fingers dove into her cunt and my thumb pressed into her clit, circling it and fucking her fast.

"Faster," she said and I went faster.

"Do it as fast as you can," she commanded and I went faster. I kissed her dark, quivering lips as I fucked her, my quick breaths breathing in hers. When she came, her head went back and her hips swung up toward me.

I sucked on her nipples while she relaxed. She kissed me in after-breaths, our sweat soaking into the sauna's bench.

Eventually, she laughed and said she had to pee. I laughed too.

"Will you be here when I get back?" she asked, suddenly a bit shy.

I said I didn't know.

She smiled, "It'll be weird when we see each other on the street." Then: "That was great," and "I've never done this before."

She planted a few kisses on me and left the sauna.

I smiled at the sudden appearance of her vulnerabilities, noticing how mine had slid away in the joy I felt when she made me make her come. I left the sauna a few minutes later dripping with heat, knowing I would beg again any day for that rush of pleasure.

Boykarleen in the Bathhouse

KARLEEN PENDLETON JIMÉNEZ

September 14, 1998

8:35 P.M. Kitchen. I casually ask my housemate, "Isn't that bathhouse thing happening tonight?" I've been in Toronto for exactly six days, living with these new housemates for two. We didn't discuss sexual politics before I moved in, and I don't want them to think I'm a slut in my first week, but I want to know if they know anything about it before I go because they seem to be the dykes-about-town. I've done research on bathhouses, asking each of my gay male friends about the corrupt adventures they have found in the steam. I envy the ease in which they caress and fuck strangers. It's easy to be bitter about the missed opportunities of my sex when they aren't possible. Now I have to know whether I can live up to my envy.

My housemate knows one of the organizers. She insists I go. "It'll be fun, Karleen, and besides, then you can tell us what happened." All three of my housemates encourage me, but none of them will go. I'm suspicious. But would I be more nervous if one of them was there? I decide there's no better opportunity to be this anonymous. Since I've arrived, I've been to one class, one soccer game, and one queer conference. How many people could I possibly recognize?

9:07 P.M. Bedroom. I line my nicest boxers along the floor and one of my housemates picks out one for me to wear. White cotton with yellow street signs over my crotch, indicating "Slippery when wet," and a navy blue muscle shirt. Is this appropriate dress for a bathhouse? I identify as butch or boy, and in true lesbian cliché fashion, I hate wearing dresses. In fact, the only time I feel like I'm dressed like a woman is when I'm naked. Therefore, I don't feel that way very often, even with my lovers. So what am I thinking bringing my body to a bathhouse?

10:05 P.M. In line. A woman makes small talk with me. I wonder if the bathhouse action begins right here. Do we start staking out prey and predators in line? There's an edge of nervousness in our conversation. If we continue with the words, if I tell her about my trip up from San Diego, the ex, the border guard, my future academic career—does this mean I've already set up expectations? Our conversation dwindles. I notice her again a few minutes later when she jumps behind me. She's dodging a big, creepy man with a Polaroid. She whispers to me that she's a computer software designer, that no one at her work knows about her sexuality. She doesn't want them to find out like this.

"It's OK. You can stand behind me for as long as you like. He can take all the pictures of me he wants." I'm out every day I walk down the street. I've got nothing to lose.

10:40 P.M. Still in line. I lose my breath for a moment when I notice my new professor standing two steps behind me. What is the etiquette for bathhouse greetings? I do my familiar Chicana raise-of-the-chin hello. Apparently it works in Canada too…but mostly we avoid looking at each other.

11:07 P.M. Still in line. A femme with a floppy dick and a velvet cape marches up and down the concrete, reassuring us that we'll get in at some point. Apparently the gay-boy owners didn't staff the place well enough for a dyke night.

11:41 P.M. The hallway. I've changed into my bathhouse outfit and am searching for a place to leave my clothes. I run smack into the professor. We look right at each other. There's no avoiding this. I didn't know earlier today, when I sat in her class for the first time, that she'd see me in my boxers a few hours later. "Welcome to Toronto," she grins. And that's it. My official welcome. I am now here in Canada.

12:32 P.M. Staircase. I've gone up and down the flights of bathhouse, from nonsmoking first to S/M fourth. Too many of the little doors are closed. The gym, where I changed clothes right before running into my professor, is now a site for fucking, only you have to be much taller than I am to see it. All of the larger rooms blind me this way. Bathhouses are hard on short people. I decide that a fire escape overlooking the pool and patio offers my best voyeur opportunities.

Two butch women strip down naked below me, then gear up harnesses and dildos and jump into the pool. All I can think is, *Do they float?*

A boy-looking girl tries to pick me up, and I get confused. In

Southern California, if you look like a boy, you mostly act like one too. But in Toronto after only a week, I'm totally disoriented. It seems like most dykes look like boys but transform into femmes after a single sentence falls from their mouths. The majority of my lovers have been femme, but while in fag moods I have on occasion sought out other butches, so I'm not opposed to the boyish look or anything. It's just that I can't even figure out what fantasy I need to make in my head to pick somebody up, because I don't know what to expect once we open our mouths. I get frustrated, and the black metal staircase feels cold beneath me. I want to give up. That's when I see the cop.

A butch god in a police shirt, boots, and a leather jockstrap pulls a blond into her crotch and rubs on her. She tugs at her roughly, then pushes her down. The blond sucks the long black cock for a while. Later, she's all legs with her ass up in the air. The butch fingers the blond's pussy now and again, testing for wetness. She smacks her ass with a hand, a whip, and a paddle, until it's all rosy. The blond wiggles her ass around. In between slaps, the cop fingers her a bit more. The blond's lips pucker out. The butch pulls out lube and a condom, applies them, and starts fucking. I mean fucking. This woman is all muscle. She looks like a jaguar or something—everything flexed, everything pulsing. Every muscle in sync, cooperating, urging the fuck to get harder, deeper, pulling all the way out, all the way in with each beat. The blond's face turns burgundy. She screams. I've never seen anything like this before. Not with women. Animals maybe, yes, like a *National Geographic* special or something. I'm watching the wilderness channel. Dykes at play in a gay-male habitat. By the barbecue, the swimming pool, a bar. The $10 cover I paid is quickly made up for with this one act.

1:15 A.M. Staircase. A butch gets fucked directly below me. I can see her through the iron grating. The black diagonal strips of metal distort the scene. The blond from earlier has reached down beneath her dildo and harness and dug inside. I know butches get fucked even if we don't readily admit it, but I'm startled to see it. Will this give me some kind of picture to be OK with myself when my girlfriend reaches for me? I watch intently and hope to memorize as much as I can. The muscles on the butch woman's face darken with a flush. Her eyes tighten. Another woman grabs at her spiked hair, jerking her neck back. She bites at the butch's throat. And yet another woman pulls up her towel to reveal a long red dildo, and nudges it at the ass of one of the others. I can't keep track of what to look at.

There's something familiar about this. My brain races to all those years of theater classes. Bathhouse sex looks like one of those human machines you build in drama class. Twenty-five people each doing a different task, a varied movement, all connected to each other in some way. There is grunting and laughing. I look back at the blond, who has pulled her fingers out and announces, "I love boys who bleed."

1:50 A.M. Staircase. A blond woman in our group of voyeurs lights a cigarette and looks mournfully over the railing. She's wearing only a towel, which gives me the chance to sneak appreciative looks at her breasts. She shakes her head. "All the ones with the dildos are getting the action. Forget the rest of us. Everyone keeps rubbing on them."

2:26 A.M. S/M floor. The rain has brought me inside. People are huddling in front of open doors. I join them, and our little mob moves along the hallway based on the intensity of the sounds emerging from the rooms. People are beginning to loosen up and let us watch.

In the corner room, a round woman is whipping another politely. I comment on this to the other onlookers. One tells me that Canadians are more polite than Americans. The woman being whipped is reddening and shaking. She leans her arm against the wall for support. She announces that she can't take anymore, and the round woman stops and caresses her. It's so tender.

Two doors over, one of the women I met at the Sunday soccer game is getting fucked. Her girlfriend grinds her fingers between her thighs, and her body jerks. She's playing the little schoolboy for the night. She has blue hair, a tool belt, a collar. I remember meeting her yesterday. I sat next to her on a bench, making small talk, watching her body, both relaxed and inviting in the afternoon breeze. I try to find that woman in the face now contorted into constant screaming.

When I meet people, I often play a game with myself in which I fantasize what they would look like in the middle of sex. I may not be attracted to them at all. I often have no motivation for the fantasy other than curiosity. What do people really look like underneath all their civility? In the past few hours, I have recognized at least 10 women I've met or seen in my six days in Canada.

3:02 A.M. S/M floor hallway. A young woman wearing a black leather miniskirt sits smoking on a bench. She was part of my voyeur group. I notice her dark, thick curls and think it would be nice to squeeze them. She has light blue eyes that glow in the black lights. Her cheeks are round, and her dimples deepen in the corners when she inhales. She is most definitely both femme and cute. I want to approach her. I can't go home without at least trying something risky and worthwhile. I ask her which room she liked the best. She grins and offers me a seat next to her. She pulls out a cigarette and hands it to me. We smoke and talk about how out of place we feel. We discuss our lives, and I tell her about how suffocating San Diego and its border are, about how good it felt to drive so many miles away. She says she's from Ottawa and had to leave because it is a city without texture.

4:15 A.M. Porn room. My new friend and I have found the porn room and are critiquing a film of two women shaving each other. Our heads tilt side to side as we try to understand what angle the camera has taken us in. The actresses sit in the bathtub giggling, clutching long straightedges against raw pink cunts. I've never seen this before. I've done it, I've just never seen it. We both cross our legs unconsciously. When the actresses get up and strut their proud, smooth pussies at us, my friend turns and asks if I've had enough of this. I offer her a ride home through the rain.

5:37 A.M. Lucy's apartment. She invites me in for tea and cookies. I don't drink tea, but I'm in Canada, after all, and want to be polite. And I've already decided for a while now that I want to kiss her. How many hours of the right conversation and smiles are necessary before I lean over and put my lips on hers? I'm envying my gay male counterparts. They've told me that the point for them is not to know the person.

Here I am still trying to establish some kind of grounds for a kiss. Does the bathhouse merely speed up lesbian processing but not eliminate it? Is it only a matter of practice, and will I get it down to two hours next time? Lucy hands me a slip of paper. I see "Lucy" scribbled next to a phone number and realize I hadn't known her name until that moment.

6:05 A.M. The street. Lucy walks me out and nervously waves goodbye. I ask if I can kiss her before she goes. The muscles around her lips loosen. She is relieved and happy. She comes closer. I walk over and pull her hips gently into mine. Her waist is soft and round, and my hand instinctively begins to stroke her. I lift my other hand and trace my fingers along her jawline. I press my lips against hers. She pushes her tongue deep into my mouth. We find a rhythm that works. The air is still wet, dripping along our skin. I imagine what we look like here, a black-and-white romance movie maybe, the irony of such a traditional end—a simple kiss and embrace against a drenched landscape at dawn.

FUCK CLUBS

Stepmaster

HILARY CELLINI COOK

I made this skirt a few years ago when I used to sing in a choir. We had to wear long black skirts and white blouses for concerts, so I made this one up in black velvet. The waist is a little tight now, but it balances out once I lace up the back on my black leather corset. The whole thing leaves me a little breathless.

My lover wants to be clear before we go. *What would we like to do? What's not OK?* But the whole thing makes me feel a little vague, incapable of decision.

She was there before, by herself, the first time they held the women's sex club in this converted Victorian house that's usually reserved for men. She described it to me on the phone when

I was 2,000 miles away, playing down the parts where she was turned on, the girl she eventually kissed. But now I'm here, and she seems so happy to be going back with me.

✠ ✠ ✠

Do we want a tour? Oh, no. We want to do this ourselves. We peek into the steam. We climb to the second-floor drawing room where women line the walls like boys at a high school dance. It's only 7:30, and no one has had enough to drink.

We climb one more flight and find the smokers and our locker, into which we jam our oversize bag. I change from twill pants and big black street shoes into my 18th-century velvet cascade and soft leather corset, which plays up my cleavage. Karleen takes off her coat. Some kind of butch prerogative means she can walk the streets in her sexiest outfit, tonight a pair of jeans, a white tank top, and an olive-green military jacket with a silver heart pinned on the sleeve where her rank should be. Without her glasses and with that razor cut she gets at Joe's Barber Shop, she looks like some clean-cut boy-child who lied about his age to get into the service, and yet I'm always amazed when people mistake her for a man. She's always looked like a beautiful dyke to me.

The stairs open out at the third floor onto a gracious landing. We didn't think there were stairs to the fourth floor until I found the tiny maid's staircase, not even wide enough for two servants to pass each other with a chamber pot. We climb to the top floor, and I pull her into a little room and shut the door. I love the dimness of this place. I love the attic warren of little rooms. I love the mirrors and the murk and the partitions that pretend to give us privacy.

Karleen always moves like she has a dick. She shudders if I run my hand along her fly. Tonight she's packing. We're lying on the bed admiring ourselves in the mirror as she moves against me. She's pulling up my skirt, undoing her jeans. I look up and see us at an angle from above: a boy soldier over a ringleted woman in a black décolleté top, one strap sliding off of her shoulder. I run my hand over the back of her neck and watch in the mirror as the woman does too, watching his urgent movements as he spreads her knees, round and white on either side of his trousers, and pushes in.

Karleen quizzes me about what I've been doing this week. We're slipping into another kind of game. People know about our unconventional relationship, but they don't know about the games it allows us to play. On Monday, it turns out, I had a date with my husband to get laid before day care closed. She needs to punish me, and I know it. She knows I'm her girl. She takes me back again and again, and yet every now and then something like this occurs. She smacks me a bit on the ass, even slaps my face; the sound rings out among the attic beams. We expect the organizers to break down the door any minute as this is not the S/M-friendly floor.

I sit on her now, moving around. We still can't get over the mirrors and the wonders of the 20-watt bulb. We look so beautiful and golden. I start weaving a transgressive fantasy. A recent discussion at a women's potluck on the subject of S/M had degenerated to the point where they decided that S/M could be permissible only between two middle-class white women and then only if they did not play with race or class.

"Race or class," I had said, when Karleen repeated this to me. "Why didn't I think of that?" I had been trying to come up with something ever since.

"How about," I say to her, sitting above her making little circles on her dick, "if I have a fantasy that I'm a maid in a Victorian house, and the youngest son comes home from boarding school in England and suddenly he's looking at me differently. He's 17." (I think Karleen would go younger, but whatever). "He follows me with his hot glances as I go about my household work. He slides a hand down the inside of my arm as I pass him in the hall."

"Do you remember how I used to care for you when you were little?" I tell him. "Even then you would run your hand over the tops of my breasts, but you were just a baby. You're not a baby now.

"That would be playing with class, don't you think?" I ask.

Karleen doesn't care. She's already that boy, home from school, making his way up to my attic room. Arrogant, innocent, exercising his class privilege, and falling into Oedipal lust all at once.

"My, how you've grown," I tell him. She's reaching up and pulling my right breast out of my corset, fondling it like she's never touched one before, drawing it to her mouth.

"There's my sweet boy—that's what you need. You're just a hungry boy." Her lips and her teeth and her palate pull on my nipple, sending electric shivers down to the part of me that's still wrapped around her dick, and I don't know how she feels it, but she does, and she shoves her dick into me, breathing harder. She's pushing into me, and the suckling baby finally loses out to the boy as she lets my breast slide out from between her teeth and begins to fuck up into me as hard as she can.

"Shh," I whisper as she moans. "Your mother will hear."

Her hands are on my hips, and she's focused and shuddering. She's searching my face for the impact of her dick at the core of me, watching for me to wince as it slams past my cervix. And I do wince. With my legs apart and her holding me in place as she thrusts, I can't escape her, I can't lessen the impact of each blow. She's going faster now, losing control, going over the top. *Oh, oh, oh. Thank you, why are you so good to me? Why do you let me use you so hard? Thank you. Oh, thank you.* We lie tangled, breathing and sweating, boy and maid, dyke and dyke.

Then she wets her fingers and reaches down to stroke me. She's no longer the arrogant boy. She's someone who knows me, who's done this before, and knows what to do. She takes my nipple between her lips, and I arch my back, pulled tight between the abrasion of her teeth on my nipple and the wetness of her fingers slipping over and over my clit. *Don't stop, don't stop, don't stop.* My body is so clenched it feels like it's going to lock into spasms, but her fingers pull it over the top, and the contractions pass through me wave on wave, warm blood radiating from the center down my legs and rising over my face. Her body falls over mine, and she holds me close. "It's OK, girl. I've got you," she murmurs.

Eventually I say, "Karleen, I don't feel so shy anymore. Let's go downstairs." The third-floor landing is packed. Half of Karleen's classmates from university seem to be there smoking and talking about their courses, professors, and the other half of their classmates. So much for anonymous sex.

We do the circuit again. Wandering through the steamy rooms and the bar on the second floor, dancing while she slides her hand up my skirt, two women smiling and pointing at the shape of her dick running up beside my baby's fly.

In the Nautilus room two women are engaged in a scene. One tenderly flogging the other, the women talking softly and giggling together. The woman being flogged is gently blindfolded and balanced on some stabilizing metal bars, as her ass gets red and her feet get sore. "Let's go in," Karleen says.

We sit at the bottom of the treadmill, watching the flogging and the tours coming through. Women jam into the corner of the corridor to watch, afraid to cross the threshold, to implicate themselves in some way, and to risk having to fight their way back through the crowd like someone who has gone too far back in the streetcar and is going to miss her stop.

"Baby, I need to punish you. You know that, don't you?" Karleen says in my ear. I feel myself blushing.

"Yes," I say. I keep looking over at the door. There aren't so many people there. Maybe three or four. Or five.

She's kissing my throat, running her finger down my collarbone, talking gently in my ear. "I think these people need to see what a little whore you are," she says, sending shivers down my spine.

"The riding crop is in the locker," I tell her. I'm the one who packed it. I give her the key out of my shirt pocket. My hands are shaking.

In a sense it is performance. In my mind's eye I can see us there, see her talking seriously in my ear, touching my bare arm, the back of my neck, my throat, my breasts resting in the top of the corset as I blush. And when she comes back, there is theater in the way she helps me up while telling me to lift my skirt and bend over the StairMaster. I rest my left foot on the pedal and it begins to move down. I rest it on the central frame instead and reach my arms up to grip the hand rails on either side. The whole time she's talking to me in a whisper.

"You let him fuck you? You let him put his dick in you? What were you thinking?" And she hits me with the crop. Hard. Harder than usual. The theater is receding, and I'm alone, just my hands gripping the metal railings, flinching when she pauses, looking in the mirror to see what she's doing with that riding crop, but not wanting her to see me doing it. I hear someone say "Oh, my God, look at her ass!" as I turn and it catches the light. Karleen is turned on, wanting to hit, not wanting to pause. My skirt slips down, and I bend down to pull it up again with one hand. My eyes are alternately squeezed shut and huge in the mirror. The crop comes again. Two, then three times on the same spot. I cry out and put my hand out to protect my ass.

"Why did you let him?" she says in my ear. "You know you're mine."

"It feels good," I say. I see her raise the crop again. I lower my head and look under my arm at the doorway, where a sudden crowd has formed, 11, 12, more, pressing in. A woman with short dark hair is standing about five feet inside the door, riveted. She looks like she's being drawn in by a hypnotic force. Her mouth is open, and in a flash I see us there, Karleen leaning over me with that concentrated look she gets, the face of a boy and the focus of a woman, and me all in black, my shoulders and arms emerging pale and round from my corset, my hands gripping that kinky machine and my ass and legs vulnerable. The eyes of strangers are almost worse than the crop.

Karleen is stroking my ass. It feels so hot. It feels so good. She's lifting me into her arms. She drops the crop. Kissing my mouth, "I love you. I love you."

I hold on to her so hard. The wool of her army jacket is rough on my bare arms. Squinting at the crowd in the doorway, not entirely sure I want to know, I feel like a little kid peeking at strangers over my mother's shoulder.

"I want to fuck you, baby." This time I try holding on to the machine again, but when she slides her wet hand into me, I discover I've lost the power to stand. When I was in early labor with my daughter, not so very long ago, I found myself slipping in the same way onto the floor of the waiting area at the birth center and resting my head on the couch. Just primal. Not a pain thing. My body is going down. It doesn't matter if I'm in the waiting room or if thousands of queer men have walked their bare feet across the acrylic carpet in this exercise room, my body is going down there.

She feels so good. Somewhere I hear a woman's voice, husky, crying out with each stroke of her hand. Karleen moves faster. I am twisting under her hand, turning sideways, and feeling my insides clamp down on her suddenly wet hand, squeaking against them. I curl up on the floor while she holds me, then I sit up and curl around her. Her jeans are soaked to the knee. "Messy girl, " she tells me affectionately. "Look at the mess you made."

Somehow we get out of there. Somehow we get through that bunch at the door and out to the smoky landing again. Everybody smoking, cruising, discussing their work, trying to get info on some woman they saw at the beginning of the evening. "You look so innocent," says Karleen. "You'd never know to look at you."

I meet a lawyer friend I'd seen earlier. Then another lawyer who starts talking about various firms. Where am I articling, she wants to know. We know even more lawyers in common. I will be running into her the rest of my life. I am demure in my long skirt and corset. Overdressed if anything. She knows nothing, I'm sure. How many people have seen it all anyway? Behind me Karleen is talking to yet another classmate. "I hear you're a bit of a voyeur," says Karleen.

"I hear you're a bit of an exhibitionist," says the classmate. Oh, damn.

I turn back to the lovely lawyer. She's looking at the black riding crop across the knees of my black skirt with her eyebrows raised.

"Karleen, let's go upstairs."

I want to get back into one of those murky attic rooms. It's late, and the high school dance effect is wearing off. In the long corridor between the front and the back of the attic naked women are kissing and fucking on the bench. I see a hand disappear between slick thighs. Farther into the warren we stand in the heat and smoke, staking out locked cubicle doors and listening. I think that one's empty, but no, the moans start, barely audible, and then louder and more urgent until they cascade over the top. Then another one from over there, and one from that corner. We are bathed in sweat and other women's pleasure. A door opens and two women stumble out. At last. But no, there are two more women in there, and they are sure as hell not finished yet. For God's sake, we have a child-care situation. We have to get home soon. Finally a couple give up their space. We rip off the sheet, happily remaking the bed. All around in the bad light women are sighing, coming, whispering.

"Listen," I say. It's the two lawyers waiting for a room. One of them has an unmistakable laugh. From another cubicle comes a sound like someone popping bubble wrap. Or slapping bare skin. I laugh into Karleen's shoulder. Open up in there, S/M police. And later, as we move together, and sigh, and make little noises of our own, I hear first one of the lawyers crying out as she comes, and then the other.

I'll see you in court, girlfriend.

I was a Pro-Dom Virgin

TRISTAN TAORMINO

I have one of the best jobs in the world. I am Adventure Girl. Adventure Girl is the title of the column I write for On Our Backs magazine. The premise is simple: The editors send me on a new sexual adventure every other month—something I haven't done before—and I share every detail of this new experience with my readers. I had already bought a lap dance at a local strip club and ventured to a swingers party in the suburbs. And for my third adventure, they decided I should visit Pandora's Box...

When the elevator door slides open on the top floor of this ordinary office building in the Flatiron District, the reception area looks like the lobby of a small upscale hotel. Lushly decorated in shades of burgundy, hunter green, and other inky hues with well-polished dark-wood furniture, the room has a sexy, gothic quality. I'm at Pandora's Box, one of New York's finest dungeons, to schedule a session with a professional dominatrix.

"Do you know what you have in mind?" asks Lara, one of the managers.

"I was thinking about some bondage, flogging, and maybe play piercing."

"Hmm…" she responds. "I'm not used to women coming in here and knowing exactly what they want. Usually if women come here at all, it's with their husbands—reluctantly."

She gives me a big leather portfolio containing photographs of all the house mistresses. I look through the pages of women in full dominatrix wear, stylized settings, dramatic poses. I was expecting there would be more to go on: some sort of bio of each of them, a list of their specialties, a brief missive, something to give me a feel for their individual personas. But, for the most part, I have only photos. I am reminded that this profession is geared toward men as I search to no avail for the fierce butch top. There's lots of lipstick and overcoiffed hair and cleavage—I mean, some of the mistresses look downright "girly," which isn't my thing.

Amidst all the femmey drag, I seek out the ones who look tough. Lara tells me that one of my choices, Isabelle, is also a manager and will be working tomorrow.

"She may be able to take a break to do a session, but you'll have to call tomorrow."

There is a flurry of activity in anticipation of a big client who's due to arrive, so I hang around for a while, hoping some of the women will come in and I can check them out in the flesh. When Mistress Sydney walks in, I know right away she's the one. After Lara introduces us, Mistress Sydney immediately tops me as she tells me to do something. She also seems genuinely eager to do a scene with a woman. It's true that probably all the women would do a scene with another woman, but, as you can imagine, some would be more into it than others.

Lara gives me a copy of the extensive information form, which all clients fill out, the house keeps on file, and the mistress reviews before each session. There are the rudimentary questions about medical problems, experience level, and pain tolerance. One section asks me to rate my interest (from 0 to 5) in various activities and the intensity level (light, medium, or heavy) I'd like to experience: spanking, flogging, caning, bondage (rope), bondage (other), slapping, humiliation, public humiliation, sensory deprivation, blindfolds, hoods, gags, mummification, straitjackets, wrestling, foot worship, kicking, nipple torture, golden showers, enemas, hot wax, rubber toys, forced feminization, cock-and-ball torture, play piercing. The next section is a list of role-playing options to check: student/teacher, mommy/child, abductor/abductee, nurse/patient, trainer/dog, mistress/slave (and some others I can't remember because I wasn't really into that part).

The final section is what you'd like your mistress to wear: leather, latex, PVC, corsets, high heels, boots, no shoes, gloves, medical, uniform (specify). When I'm finished with my form, it's all there on paper—all my desires tabulated and rated. No one has to do any guesswork, not even me. I return it to Lara, who gives me an appointment for the next day.

When I arrive for my session, Isabelle greets me at the door. I recognize her from the portfolio, although she's much more beautifully striking than her photos. Tall and slender with chin-length golden hair, she looks refined, assured, experienced, and a little severe. She's dressed in a black suit, her jacket classic, tailored, but the skirt is more daring—short, slightly shimmery. Her long legs ending in superhigh patent leather heels. She would make a perfectly demanding teacher or a strict equestrian trainer with a serious riding crop. My fantasies are already in full swing.

As I tour the different rooms, I'm struck at how elaborately and thoughtfully each one is decorated and equipped. The "Role-Play Room" has lots of different enclaves: the colorful, majestic carousel horse (for mommy/kid scenes) and a vanity and mirror with drawers of cosmetics and wigs (good for cross-dressing and "forced feminization"). The classroom has a blackboard and little desks with attached chairs, and around the corner is a black vinyl bondage table leaning against a wall full of whips, floggers, canes, and leather restraints. The "Versailles Room" is actually two rooms decorated in the style of 18th-century French aristocracy—lots of plush couches and chairs, an ornate chandelier, a thronelike chair on a raised platform fit for a queen. It reminds me of an upper-class lady's boudoir.

The next room is "The Dungeon," which is pretty self-explanatory: wooden stockades, a bondage table, a wrought-iron cage, an eerie-looking coffin, and some sort of sawhorse apparatus. The Dungeon feels noticeably cooler than the other rooms.

Mistress Sydney's long, curly hair is pulled back loosely. She's dressed in an outfit similar to when I saw her last night: black silky, clingy pants, high heels, and a black lace bustier. She has off-white chiffon skin and dark, perfectly lined lips.

"Hi, how are you?" she says, pleased to see me, smiling genuinely, holding my questionnaire in her hand.

"I'm nervous," I admit.

She reviews my questionnaire with me, asking me a question every now and then, commenting, nodding, taking mental notes.

"So, you'd like a 'little' public humiliation, right?"

"Um, yeah…" I giggle.

"Now, what about humiliation in private?"

"Well, I like to be told what to do, given orders, disciplined. I suppose it's more discipline than humiliation. Sometimes I can be a wiseass and need to be put in my place."

"Very good." Pause. "What kind of sensory deprivation do you prefer?"

"Blindfolds, mostly, I guess. Maybe a gag, but not a hood or earplugs."

She nods, then reads aloud to herself. "Play piercing, good … 5 for slapping, good…hot wax, you're not really into."

She reminds me that penetration and sexual acts of any kind are illegal and not part of the services provided. She tells me that my safeword is "mercy," but I must use it properly, as in "Mercy, Mistress, please."

"Would you like to have an enema to start?" she asks. Now, she doesn't know I wrote a book on anal sex, so this question immediately makes me think she's got me pegged. I agree.

She leads me to the "Medical Room," where our scene will take place, which is mirrored on all four walls and the ceiling. A white vinyl table sits in the middle of the room with white leather restraining straps, white leather wrist and ankle restraints, and metal stirrups at one end. Glass shelves with glass jars of medical paraphernalia line one wall. In the corner sits a tank of oxygen and an IV stand. A white leather hood hangs on a hook to the left of the sink. There are white cabinets everywhere. She tells me to get fully undressed, and she leaves the room.

So there I am, totally naked, surrounded by my reflection, already feeling at a disadvantage. When Sydney returns with a handful of floggers and a paper bag stuffed full, she tells me to get on my hands and knees on the table. She fills a clear IV bag with water, and I feel tubing slide inside my ass. She's careful, gentle. The water pressure is very low, but I quickly feel myself filling up, and I say something to that effect.

"You can take it," she says, reassuring but firm. "Hold it like a good girl."

And I do until I feel like I'm going to burst, and say, "Mistress, I feel like I have to go." She instructs me to walk naked through the lobby to the bathroom.

When I return to the room, she tells me to bend over the table with my ass in the air.

"I'm going to invite my friend, another mistress, in here to spank you."

I can't see who comes in with her, don't want to turn all the way around to try because that would be disrespectful. I imagine that it's Isabelle. The second mistress runs her hands up and down my back and legs. She slaps my ass, and her touch is firm, deliberate. They talk about me as the spanking continues, and mistress Sydney tells me I'm being punished for not taking the whole enema bag. She also tells me I'd better take the spanking and not make her look bad in front of another mistress. The spanking gets progressively harder, and they talk about how when the second mistress starts to hit me with more force, I let out a squeak.

"I like that sound she makes," cackles the second mistress. "I want to hear it again. This little bottom of yours is adorable and so sweet, Sydney."

My ass becomes so raw and the smacks feel so intense that I'm convinced she must have switched to a leather paddle at some point. She can't possibly hit me this hard with her bare hand. Mistress Sydney then ties my hands with rope and some very skilled knot work.

When she's finished with the knots, she says, "Ask nicely for more. I know you want to."

I think I'm nearing my limit, so I say, "Please, can I have a *little* more, Mistress?" They both giggle and tell each other how cute and well-behaved I am (as if I'm not even there).

Mistress Sydney unties my wrists and tells me to turn over and lie on my back. I do, so now I'm staring at my naked body in the mirror on the ceiling. I also see then that it is not Mistress Isabelle who's been making my ass cheeks burn, but a mistress I saw last night; she was in a white latex minidress and nurse's cap carrying a black medical bag. I recognize her from the big leather book: it is Mistress Maxim, whose nickname is Mad Max. She has a mane of red hair the color of Cajun seasoning, dark lips, and a sinister look in her eye.

"Have you ever played with clothespins?" Mistress Sydney asks.

"No," I answer honestly.

"But you can take them, can't you?" It's sort of a rhetorical question.

Mistress Sydney tells me to spread my legs, then they both go to work on me. I feel fingers squeezing sections of my pussy lips, then the pressure of a clothespin clipping the flesh. As more clips are added, the sensations build until I am over-whelmed with stimulation. I can't tell exactly what's going on, what they are doing to me. Four hands travel over my labia, my opening, my bush, my asshole. When they brush against a clothespin, I feel a surge in my pussy. They seem to be nudg-ing the clips one at a time, then a few at a time, until I am reel-ing from the stimulation.

I feel a clothespin press on my clit, then another. The wood-en clips pinch little pockets of flesh surrounding my asshole. The clips are adding so much pressure to my clit, I feel like I'm going to explode. I imagine they are sliding clips inside me, in my pussy and ass, and once they are inside, they press the ends together and I feel two wooden pegs open, filling me up and stretching me at the same time.

"Mistress Sydney," I say, "may I come, please?"

"Yes, you may," both mistresses answer in unison.

And I do. I start to breathe in short bursts and my muscles tighten until my orgasm washes over me. When my breathing slows down, Mistress Max starts to remove the wooden clamps. As each one comes off, I feel a seething pain in my pussy. While the blood rushes back to my parts, they comfort me, tell me I'm a good girl, tell me they know it hurts, that it hurts the worst when they come off.

When the last one is off, Mistress Max cups my mound in her hand. I feel like I need an ice pack or a cold compress or something, but when she takes her hand away, it feels a lot better. Mistress Max leaves the room. Mistress Sydney stands above me, strokes my head, talks in soothing tones.

I don't know how long I'm spinning on a high—high from submission, high from the pain and endurance, high from the release of coming. When I come down from it, she's still there.

"We didn't get to do everything on your list, but I hope you enjoyed your experience."

I sit up, still naked and dazed, and blurt out a million questions. How did you get into this? How long have you been doing it? How long have you worked here and where else have you worked? What do you like and dislike about it? What's the difference between topping a man versus a woman?

"Send all the lesbians you know to me," she says, and she is sincere.

I tell her that if I get a good royalty check soon, I will definitely be back to see her. And this time, I can leave my notepad at home and concentrate on her sumptuous breasts spilling out of the bustier and her voice, stern but warm. *Mercy, Mistress, please.*

F ETISH

Bathtub Girl & Psychobitch

TRIXI

I stepped over a melting, ant-covered raspberry lollipop and a mound of spent matches into Virgil's Used Books. Virgil brought new depth to the word *used*. The Weeble-shaped, unbathed, stringy-haired owner looked up at me and said, "I have a book. A book for you, lady." He trolled a dusty pile to his left like a demonic dentist grubbing for scraps of gold, found the book, tucked it in his sweaty armpit, and shuffled over.

Virgil knew my taste: dingy, existential, hot. He walked back behind the counter, clearing his raspy throat and running his paint-stained hand along the underside of the grimy counter-top. "Here, lady," he coughed, laying the book ever so gently on the counter. "*The Last Stand of Mr. America*. I saw it and knew you had to have it. Had to. This one. You should buy this one."

So I did.

An hour later I slid into my steaming after-work bath with a mug of cold sun tea, holding the book above the bubbles as I readjusted the deflating bath pillow.

Within 15 minutes I found myself lying listlessly in the abstract fist of *The Last Stand of Mr. America*. Sex clubs. Self-exploration. Dirty bathrooms. Lost souls. The intensity excited and relaxed me.

I heard a knock at the door. "Honey," my girlfriend, Crystal, said. "I know you hate when I disturb you in the bath, but I need to grab the hair clippers."

"Come on in."

Crystal gently cracked open the door, letting a crisp slice of cold air in. "Jesus, you're gonna develop varicose veins in water that hot. Oh—sorry. Do not disturb. Shh…" She slipped her hand into the side vanity drawer and grabbed the dusty clippers with their one-inch attachment. The door timidly clicked shut.

There was a time, a year or so ago, when she would have climbed in the tub. There was a time when I wouldn't have minded. But now I need my hour alone, shriveling to my future, reading semipornographic literature, watching my cat lick the flat bubbles from the edge of the tub.

I heard Crystal flip on the clippers, mowing her hair to a perfect inch, as she did every weekend. The tips glittering with red-dye residue like bloodstained grass. I love the way it bristles. The cut emphasizes her amazing hazel eyes and perfect cheekbones. And her soft lips, perfectly manicured eyebrows, and a friendly little mole she calls Bob.

I turned back to my book where our main character, a bleak, intimacy-damaged fag looking for lust in all the right places, was about to bone a tranny. I'm so hot I don't even dry off. I drop the book on the cheap linoleum and hop out to find my girl-friend…*leaving*.

"See ya. I'm off to Caroline's." Caroline's—where they'll listen to her roommate's new CD, smoke Camels, drink beer, and talk about the woes of not having cable. With me here, dripping on the carpet, reading my fuck-boy books, waiting to vibrate with my consolation prize.

I stepped back into the tub, trying to refresh it with a nice jet of heat—but the heat was tapped. Sighing, I climbed out, headed into the bedroom, and reached for my Wahl Wonder tucked not-so-subtly into a velvet bag.

I lay down on the edge of the unmade bed, flicked on my handheld mistress and buzzed away. My scenario was quick: walking into a bathroom stall at a bar. A huge crack between the stall divider and the wall allows me to peek next door where a thin young man with a sunken chest and redder-than-life lips is leaning back uncomfortably on the damp, cigarette-scarred toilet lid. A slightly older, long-haired man takes the huge cock of Red Lips in his mouth.

Red Lips is too inexperienced to take charge. He rocks back and forth, trying not to come. Closing his eyes, biting his lip, taking in only small puffs of air.

"Bend over," the long-haired one orders.

Red Lips turns around, spreads his hands on the wall and bends down just out of my view to take a cock up his tight ass. He bangs up and back against the wall, grimacing and moaning…

I buzz on and on in small circles, careful not to let it go too fast. I hope I can ejaculate. I love the feeling of heat streaming from my body.

The fantasy fades away, and I focus solely on my orgasm, which came so intensely that I jerked up to a sitting position, where I hung, catching my breath.

✠ ✠ ✠

I finished my book in four baths, a faster-than-average time. By the end of it I found myself obsessed with the idea of being a gay man rubbing my cock shamelessly while a roomful of horny men roam around, each begging to suck me off. I bring the fantasy into reality, settling on the idea of pushing my strap-on hard into a dyke bent over in a dank, used back room of some skank dive. Now, how to break this to my girlie?

"Crystal, did you know there's a group of queer men called the O Boys whose sole purpose is to organize orgies? That's what they do while we're playing pool and fixing potlucks."

"Oh, that's not true. That's just a tiny little bunch of horny guys. I'm sure there are women out there who do that kind of thing too. And we've never been to a potluck—at least use stereotypes from this decade," she said as she popped open her third Pepsi of the day. Her bedtime Pepsi.

"Do you ever think about doing something a little sceney?" I asked while she surfed our five fuzzy TV stations.

"What do you have in mind?" Crystal cooed, moving closer to me. Always ready.

"Sex clubs."

"Sex clubs? Sounds scary. You know I'm Class-A Butch Bait." Then she turned back to her Pepsi and the empty TV.

"What if I found some place crazy and hot?"

"Sure," she said, thinking I was just rambling on with no intention of ever following through (as had been my pattern). "Did you tape *The X-Files* this week? Nothin's on now…"

Over the next week I scanned every paper, magazine, leather-shop flyer ledge, and college radio station—then I found it: the Annual Fetish Ball, hosted by Angel and Vampiress Divain. Vinyl, leather, PVC, drag, straight, dommes, slaves, live spanking shows, theater performances, bondage, films, and a dungeon. Perfect.

"I found it. You and I have a date. Next Saturday," I said as I walked straight by Crystal and into the bathroom. I cranked on the water.

"What?" I heard her ask from the hallway.

"I'm taking you to a dungeon. Fetish Ball. Next Saturday. 9 P.M. Now kiss me before I begin the ritual…"

She pushed open the door, rolled her eyes, kissed me on the head, and left. I hopped into the bathtub, this time reading *The Lesbian Guide to S&M*.

✠ ✠ ✠

By next Saturday Crystal was beside herself. She had dyed her hair three times, ultimately settling on a bleached white, had her eyebrows done, and fretted about whether to wear the dog collar or the silver chain.

"Dog collar, honey," I said. "Calm down. We need a drink before the festivities or you're gonna pop open."

"Not without permission," she smiled coyly, getting in the mood.

We left around 8:30, stopping by Maverick's for a quick prune vodka and beer. Yes, prune vodka. It tastes good. Really.

Crystal wore a see-through dress made of black spiderwebs. She looked amazing. Pink nipples lurking just beneath the sheer fabric. Shaved and oiled body. Tea tree lotion. Trimmed nails. I eventually decided on vinyl pants with a sheer shirt borrowed from a fashionable fag.

Maverick's wiggled with its usual crew: the old Indian bartender who sang Frank Sinatra on karaoke nights, the drag queen with the bad hair, the thin black man who always brought a new belligerent alcoholic with him, the aging leather son without a daddy, the trio of boys who dropped quarters for the Spice Girls and ABBA all night, and the average queers. Everyone greeted us with friendly catcalls and free beer.

Crystal ducked into Maverick's bathroom halfway through her beer, figuring the line at the Fetish Ball would be outrageous (and potentially scary). I followed her in, watching the way her dress clung to her bare ass. My boot stopped the door from shutting. She smiled up and let me in.

I locked the door then pushed her roughly against the back wall, squeezing her nipples with a slight twist until I heard her suck in a mouthful of air. I sat her up on the waist-high countertop and told her to lean back against the mirror.

"I want you dripping wet," I told her.

"I am…"

"More. Use your fingers."

She sucked on her fingers for a minute, then hiked up her dress and inserted them just inside. Crystal loves being fucked, and I knew her fingers wouldn't do. Forcing her to tease herself always got me hot.

"I want you to do it," she whined.

"No. Rub yourself if you can't get enough."

"You know I can't," she moaned.

Can't come without me, I smiled.

"How wet are you?"

"Please. I'm so wet. I'm ready. Please…"

I knelt in front of her while she pulled at my hair. Then I changed my mind. "Let's go. We'll finish later."

"That's not fair—" she started, but I cut her off by grabbing her throat in my hand and squeezing.

"What?" I asked.

"Nothing," she said with wide eyes. "Nothing." It was the first time I'd been this rough with her.

"Let's go."

"Please…" she begged, her head down, staring at my prick. "Please let me suck you off. Please—"

"Why?"

"We both can get off." Because she can actually come without being touched.

"No. I don't want to get off. I want you to, but *only* when I tell you to. And I said *not right now.*"

"Fuck you," she cursed.

I grabbed her by the neck again and pushed her up against the mirror again. "What? What did you say?"

Now there was genuine fear in her eyes. "Nothing. Let me go."

I fed on my anger, reached down with my left hand to let my strap-on free. Without losing eye contact, I slid inside her and rocked so hard she crashed against the mirror, almost breaking it.

"Don't make a fucking noise or I'll stop," I hissed.

She only nodded, beginning to feel the first wave of an orgasm. I tightened my grip on her throat. Her face reddened.

"Harder? You want me to fuck you harder?" I whispered.

"Yes."

She spoke. I pulled out.

"No." Then she just shook her head, eyes pleading, hands grabbing my hips.

"No noise," I said.

She nodded vigorously and even held her hands up against the wall as if she were restrained. I pushed hard and fast inside her, fucking deeper with each bump until I thought she'd tear open.

Instead she came and came again. Quiet as night. Wetter than a can of Coke in the Texas sun, as my uncle used to say.

Then we washed our hands and left, each of us thankful that since this was primarily a boy bar, there was no line of overbearing dykes waiting outside. Now, on to the Fetish Ball...

✠ ✠ ✠

We parked on Hollywood Boulevard where the commercial freaks hang out. Crystal held her jacket closed despite the warm breeze. As we approached the line to the Fetish Ball, she loosened her grip, realizing that no one else shared her modesty. PVC rave fags with five-inch glittering nails and pancake makeup...men walking on all fours, red marks slicing across their bare, hairy asses, their dominatrix-masters barking commands…women poured into their rubber suits, breasts spilling out of the top…dungeons and dragons men with long braided hair and bullwhips…leather Renaissance wenches…pansexual Marilyn Manson clones…steel, tattoos, masks, gloves, smoke.

We each paid our $20 and slowly moved in behind a pair of shirtless queers. One wore a bull's ring through his septum, the other had needles running through two-inch slabs of flesh on his back. They had matching brands on their shoulders: the letter X.

Crystal read the schedule and floor plan on the wall, immediately deciding she wanted to watch the theater performance at midnight and do a little dancing on the fourth floor. Maybe, maybe wander down to the catacombs in the basement.

After waiting 20 minutes to get a drink at the bar, then another 10 to make it up the looping, crowded stairways to the fourth floor, we found the dance floor nearly empty. Three gothic girls and an angry NIN man with fangs.

"I wonder if they're real," Crystal whispered loudly to me.

"I don't know, but I think *those* are." I nodded to a man passing by with baby horns protruding out of the top of his scarred head.

And we noticed people looking at us—or, more specifically, looking at Crystal, whose body glowed through the thin meshing under the fluorescents. A man gave us his card, telling us to call if we ever needed a slave.

A woman leaned over the railing around the foggy dance floor and had her ass slapped red by a powerful-looking man in leather pants. A few rave kids skipped onto the floor with bottles of water and skinny legs sweating inside black and blue rubber. I yawned.

"Let's take a little stroll down to the catacombs," I said.

Crystal eyed me cautiously. "OK."

We wound back around the dimly lit stairs past the theater level and red-carpeted lobby-bar into the catacombs. Harsh, slow electronic music coaxed us into the dark hallways. Strobe lights flashed from the end of one of the paths; we opted for the other route. Thin green lights streaked across the air, as if we had stepped into *Mission Impossible.*

Crystal lit a cigarette after she smelled someone else's smoke from inside one of the tiny rooms lining the hall. Past these four rooms were two large rooms with huge glass windows in front. Play rooms.

A small crowd had gathered at each window. A tall black man wearing nothing but leather shorts pulled out his thick cock and pumped it without shame. A woman in front of him peeked back, smiled, and turned around, then reached back to give him a hand. We moved to the other window for fear of having our outfits dirtied.

A used, flabby man with a cord wrapped around his shriveled member was bending over a wooden horse, receiving tremendous cat-o'-nine-tail blows to his already reddened ass. The whipper was a burly man in his late 30s. Eyeliner. Bald head with an eagle tattoo on the slick side. Evil grimace.

This did nothing for me, though Crystal's eyes dilated a bit. We moved on past more displays: exhibitionist straight couple on a couch in one room…androgynous kneeler sucking off a young, shaven tweaker…huge woman towering over a very small man, shoving her enormous breasts in his face…two bull dykes in the corner with matching leather hats confidently checking out all the women.

I leaned against the wall in a quiet, secluded corner at the end of the hallway. "Lord, this is weird. It's almost too accepted by everyone to be hot. I don't know," I said.

"Yeah." Crystal reached up behind me, against the black wall. "What's this?"

It was a black doorknob. She turned it, and we stepped backward into a utility closet filled with buckets and mops and Green Machine by the caseload. The only light came from a small, powerful clock radio on the top of the metal shelving unit. The place smelled like wet cigarettes.

Crystal grabbed a mop handle and swung it around, inches from my face. "Who the fuck are you?" she said.

"What?"

"Look, I don't have any money. I just come in and do a little cleanup after the shows. I don't know what you want but…" Her voice fizzled.

Oh. I grabbed the mop and ripped it violently from her hands then spun it around and pressed it against her neck, pinning her to the wall. "I don't want much, not really."

Then without warning she kicked my shin. Hard. Hard enough to make me yelp and drop the mop.

"What the fuck!" *Psychobitch.*

"Fuck you!" she screamed, and for a moment I thought she'd snapped. She picked up a metal dustpan and came at me with it, hard-core.

I barely dodged her, spinning around, looking for something to defend myself with. Meanwhile she came at me again, this time making contact with my right shoulder. Now I was pissed.

I grabbed her arms roughly and pushed her to the ground. With one hand firmly rooted in her hair, pulling it back enough to make her cry out, I grabbed a dusty piece of broken glass from one of the shelves.

"Shut up," I told her with a yank. "Suck my dick."

"Fuck you," she spat.

I pulled her head around roughly until she gingerly took my cock from my pants and started moving it around inside her mouth. I felt myself getting hot from my stomach down to the middle of my thighs. Everything tensed.

I let my hold loosen on her hair as she deep-throated me but kept the glass held against her cheek. She yanked down my pants and reached her hand behind the strap-on to finger me. I felt her push against the soft spot inside as she took more and more of me inside her mouth.

Then I came, nearly falling forward, dropping the glass, dizzy with pleasure. She held on to my leg as I was calming down, rocking gently and allowing herself to go.

She smiled up at me, face still blushing with pleasure. "Let's walk home."

"My pants are filthy," I smiled. "Yeah, let's walk home…and take a bath."

Afters

ALICE BLUE

Mr. Brown called just as I was putting away the last of the toys. Don't know why I answered it, must be this "evidence" Nina keeps slapping me with. Still, clients like Brown keep the dollars coming in, and as we had this fuckin' great phone bill stuck to the fridge with a fancy magnet, I like to think that it was my wallet and not…well, not any other reason I picked up the damn phone.

He'd masturbated. It took a couple of rote repetitions of "I asked you not to call me after hours, slave," "How dare you interrupt your mistress, worm," and even a "Do you want me to be displeased?" before he finally spilled it (no pun intended) and I remembered he wasn't supposed to wank till our next session on Wednesday. I was tired, so I really didn't put that much work into my solution: "Stick a candle up your ass for 20 minutes, and don't you dare touch your dick till I tell you to."

I didn't wait for an answer, just clicked it off during his "yes, Mistress" ramble. Deep breath, deep breath. It wasn't that dealing with clients like Brown was tough, it was just that it had a been a very, very long week and the one thing that had kept me through the endless whippings, the countless clothespins, the God knows how many "Now you can jerk off, slave" routines, was the thought of hanging up my toys and getting out that door.

Then the phone rang. Two things ran through my mind as I hung up my prized Jay Marston flogger: One was Nina looking at me smugly as I tried to explain why I was late, and the other was having to scrape together enough coins to pay my bills.

In the end, dollars won and, with a theatrical sigh, I picked up the phone. Mr. Red was having a fashion crisis. For the manager of a high-end realty company with a wife, three kids, and a ridiculous mortgage, he certainly sounded like a tweaking queen. It took a little work, more of the old routine, till I got him to breathe deeply and tell me what the problem was. When he told me, I tried really hard not to laugh into the receiver: It doesn't keep up the image of Mistress Divine, Slave Master Extraordinare, when you laugh at your clients… at least not with a high-pitched squeal of childish delight rather than a bass rumble of maniacal glee.

In the end I told Red to calm down ("slut") and to just ("you silly girl") use panty hose instead of his torn fishnets ("and don't bother Mommy at work again"), and then gratefully hung up.

The dungeon was quiet. It was nice, but something nicer was waiting for me back at our little apartment. I checked my watch and gasped: I had a little over a half an hour till I was due home. Damn, Nina would be real pissed if I was late. I took a quick scan of the room, checking out the stocks, the massage table, the sling, the toy box, and all the rest—trying to see what I had to put away and what of that could wait till Saturday and my next client. Unfortunately, I still had to wipe down the table, the sling, and the braces of the cross with hydrogen peroxide—at least a 15-minute job.

I was 10 minutes into it when the phone rang again. No domestic money worries this time, I thought of Nina—and Nina scowling and pacing back and forth, and picked it right up.

Mr. Yellow this time. I swallowed my first reflexive "shit" and snapped him a sharp, "How dare you call your mistress? Didn't I say you were never to call her after 6 o'clock?" and so forth, trying to get a quick, humble apology and a hang-up.

No dice. Mr. Yellow needed help. Running the mantra of *pays the bills, pays the bills, pays the bills,* I dropped the hostility and switched to bored concern: "What is it this time, slave?"

At least Yellow was a lot more forthcoming. His Prince Albert was really inflamed and sore, it seemed. Calmly, dropping Mistress Divine enough to show concern, but not too much— after all, he had to listen to me—I told him to clean it carefully and put some Neosporin on it and call me in another day or so with a report on how it was doing.

That was it, right there: Mistress Divine was CLOSED, she had spun the sign around, put out the cat (metaphorically), and locked the door behind her.

She was going home—home to a very well deserved, and much needed, relaxing evening with her precious Nina.

✠ ✠ ✠

I was lucky, damn lucky, that she was in a good mood when I walked in the door. "Hard day at the office?" she said, handing me a cold drink after I'd shucked my coat.

I tried not to smile, tried to keep my face still as I accepted the glass and sipped it. After a nice swallow I handed it back and slowly got down on my knees before her: "Yes, Mistress. Sorry I'm late, Mistress."

"I understand, slut, but that doesn't mean you shouldn't have to be punished."

"Yes, Mistress," I said, feeling smaller, more fragile, younger—but more and more precious by the moment. "I understand."

"Good. I'm glad you do," she said with a delightful touch of sarcasm, walking up to me and putting a hand under my chin. Lifting my head, she looked into my eyes, searching my irises. "Now take off your clothes and meet me in the bedroom."

✠ ✠ ✠

My world was usually black leather, rubber, latex, and sometimes surgical steel. It was full of cowering men, boot kissing, and endless days of hearing "Yes, Mistress." I enjoyed it, and it was something I was good at, but it wasn't me.

At the doorway, I kicked off my shoes, pulled off my sweatshirt, unsnapped my bra, shucked my pants, and threw my panties in a far corner. Our place was small but not tiny; it had light, charm, and a surprisingly big bedroom. It had to have that, because our brass bed wasn't small.

That bed was our world, our oasis, our temple, our sanctuary. Looking at it, I was filled with a warm glow, a sense of having arrived. I was home, home with my mistress.

I felt her hand on the square of my back, a gentle touch. "You are my precious, but you were also late and you know how much I dislike you being late."

The venom in her words was a sour-candy performance, but as always it touched me down very deep. I wasn't going to be punished: I was wanted, desired, loved.

"Yes, Mistress," I said, turning and bowing my head. "I understand."

"You know what to do. Get ready."

I went to the bed, climbed onto its thick cloud of comforters. I stretched out, facedown in the mountain range of pillows, and spread my legs just a bit.

"You are mine, slut. You know that—you belong to me. You are mine to play with, to use for my pleasure, and to hurt if I need to. But you also know that I'm here with you, that I will always treat my favorite toy very well."

"Yes, Mistress," I said, turning my head slightly. "I understand."

"So, slut, how many minutes were you late?"

I hadn't noticed it in my rush to get home. My mind raced, so I guessed: "Fifteen minutes, Mistress."

"Wrong, slut," Nina said, kneeling beside me on the bed. "It was 20. So, for you, 25. Twenty for each minute you were late, and five for not keeping track."

"Yes, Mistress," I said, already feeling my body start to respond to the ritual, the performance, to being home with Nina—my owner.

"I think the flogger tonight," she said, getting up and moving to the toy chest, our personal toy chest. Turning my head to bury my face in the comforters, I heard the hinges squeak, heard the tumble of leather, and then the lid slowly shutting.

"Twenty-five." The first was light, a warm-up. The heavy strands of the leather flogger fell almost gently across my ass. Their touch was electric, almost shocking. I felt a body thrill race up my spine. The next touch was harder, more focused, and I felt the muscles of my ass tense just afterward, anticipating the next, harder blow.

One after another, each stroke of the whip gaining intensity, power, force…to call it pain would be a half-truth. Nina was good, very good, and the escalation of her whipping was carefully orchestrated. It was a massage at first, the strands beating down on my ass with a glorious tempo, but soon it became deeper, harder, and I started to…drift. Part of my mind was there, on that great bed, having my ass whipped, but another part of me was floating high above, entranced by the bodily sensations she was driving through me.

Harder, harder, harder—my back arched, my ass tensed, my hands clawed at the bedspreads. My breathing grew faster, faster, faster, as each stroke landed heavier. There was pain, but there was also ecstasy—and both of them were amazing.

Then it was done. My ass throbbed rhythmically, matching my hammering heartbeat. My breath was ragged, each intake, each exhale, charged with a quavering excitement. I was aware, distantly, that my cunt was very, very wet.

"Good, slut, very good. You took your punishment well—very well indeed. I would almost think you enjoyed it."

"Yes, Mistress," I said, panting heavily.

"Ah, but then you are a slut, aren't you? So of course you enjoyed it, didn't you?"

"Yes, Mistress, I enjoyed it. I enjoyed it very much."

"So show me, slut. How me how much you enjoyed it."

Yes…yes, I wanted to show her. Very much I wanted to show her.

Slowly, I rolled over, gasping as my ass rubbed gently across the stitched comforter, until I could see her: Nina stood beside the bed, still in her jeans and T-shirt, her small, hard tits visible through the thin material, nipples twin dark points that instantly made my mouth water.

"Show me, slut. Show your Mistress."

I spread my legs, cautiously, feeling the muscles in my ass strain against the movement, until they were wide open. Then I put my fingers down to my cunt lips and pulled them apart, feeling my wetness in all its throbbing glory. "See, Mistress?"

"Yes, slut, I do see. I see your very red, very wet lips; I see your clit, so big and hard, twitching with a hunger for my tongue, my touch. I see you—I see my slut."

I was flowing and could feel my clit pulsing deep and primordially down among the folds of my labia.

"I know what you want, slut. I know you too well. I know you want my lips down there between your hard thighs, you want my tongue to flicker across that little hard bead. But that's not going to happen, slut. No, not at all. Instead, I want you to show me, demonstrate for your Mistress just how big a slut you are. Show me, girl; put a hand down there and feel yourself. Touch that beating bead in your cunt. Come for me, slut; come for me good and hard."

I did. With her eyes smiling at me, I put my right hand down between my sweat-slick thighs and touched, at first, the hard point of my clit. That first contact was as shocking as the initial touch of her whip, as if a spark had jumped from my quivering finger to the pinpoint of my burning desire.

Then I really did: tapping, circling, stroking, I fell into my regular rhythm, my self-performance of jerking off. The actions may have been familiar, but the heat was tremendous, blistering—not just because of the whip, not just because of the words but because she was watching me. My wonderful mistress was watching my fingers dance and stir my molten cunt.

For her, because of her, I came—a body eruption, a wild explosion of quivering muscles. Against my will, my eyes closed, my legs closed suddenly around my hand, my throat opened, and I cried out—a deep, throaty bellow of release and joy.

"Such a good slut," my mistress said, stripping and climbing into the bed next to me, mixing her glowing heat with mine. "Such a wonderful, wonderful, slut."

Before slipping into a good sleep, I pulled myself next to her—content, happy, and glowing: I was a very good slut; and for my mistress I was the best slut in the whole world.

Collared

MEGHAN MAURY

We're meeting tonight. I haven't seen her in two weeks. I go into the bar. It's noisy and jam-packed. I don't know how I'll ever find her. I'm not sure I want to anyway. Things have been different lately. I decide to sit down on a stool, order a beer, and wait for her to find me.

I remember when we met. I was still a girl and she was still a boi. I remember the day I became hers. I was so happy. I can still taste it.

You held the knife steady running over my back like an extension of your fingertips the tension was all my own the first pierce of skin releasing knotted muscles blood and adrenaline seep from the gaps lined up and down my back three small incisions near my neck fear and com-

plete calm falling out of my brain and into my body my wrists and ankles bound, but I couldn't move even if they weren't paralyzed by sensation longer cuts shorter breaths and my body is struck with an angst I've never known I've forgotten how to breathe the cuts are breathing for me I don't want you to stop I want you to leave me scarred from head to toe from ankle to wrist from front to back over and under I want to feel every inch of my body through your knife I want more and then you stop you call me your baby boi and tell me how well I've done I have earned your respect I have earned the right to call you daddy I have earned my collar you cut me loose and make my body shake I wake up the next morning and walk through our first apartment our first city our first meeting place and I can feel the cuts with every movement pain sometimes pleasure mostly our secret people touch and they don't know that they are feeling your knife still in my skin they don't hear the intake of breath don't see the slight wince don't know I am your boi completely.

But now things aren't the same. I still have my collar, but I no longer deserve it. I wish she could see that. She loves me too much now. She has, over the years, become increasingly afraid to cause me pain. Of all people, she should understand what's been happening. I am losing my respect for her. Even now I sit here waiting for her but searching for someone else. Someone who will give me a collar I can wear with pride instead of out of habit. I'm even starting to question whether I should be bottoming at all.

I finish my beer and order another.

She takes me out, collared, and I still flirt. Why shouldn't I? I feel no need to do her bidding. I know she won't say anything while we're out. Somehow she's even gotten shy about that. And I know that when we get home my punishments will be mild if anything. We'll have a quick spat and then fuck out our frustrations.

Maybe she's stopped caring enough to discipline me. Where the hell is she anyway? We were supposed to meet at 9, and now it's almost 9:30. I don't know why I even came tonight. I sure as hell don't know why I came collared. I should have met her somewhere quiet and returned her collar so we can have both move on.

But the answer to those questions is simple. I still love her. Still want her. But we can't be together if things are going to be like this. I should just go. Instead I wait here on this stool, getting frustrated and angry. Wishing things were the way they used to be. Wishing I could go back to the days when we had fun together. When we were bois together. Fuck it. I'm tired of this.

I take out my wallet, leave some money on the bar, then accidentally drop it as a slide off the stool. Damn. I'm always clumsy when I drink. I drop to one knee to retrieve it. Before I can stand back up, a boot comes down on the center of my back, pushing my upper body closer to the floor.

"Where the fuck do you think you're going, brat?" Dani's words wrap around my wrists and ankles, binding me to my current position as adequately as any of our restraints could have.

I know she is trying. This could lead into some great sex. But I'm still pissed. And I *am* a brat.

"Home. You're fucking late." She releases some of the pressure on my back, but her foot still rests too heavily for me to move.

"What did you say? I don't think I heard you correctly." I feel her body coming closer. Smell the same cologne she has worn for four years.

"I said I'm going home. Get the fuck off me, *sir*." I feel her boot leave my back as her hands pull me into a kneeling position. I feel the sting on my right cheek before I realize she's hit me.

"Don't you ever speak to me like that again, boi. Ever. Do you understand?" The words are right, but I'll be damned if I'm going to let this erase a year of her being distant.

"Fuck you."

"What was that?"

"*Fuck you, sir.*"

"Wrong answer, brat." She reaches behind my neck, removing my collar in one swift movement. "I should have taken this away from you long ago."

She holds the collar inches from my face, dangling it between two fingers. My mind is racing. Half of me wishes she would just put the collar in her pocket, walk out, leave me here. But the other half wants this so badly. Tonight she has no shame about commanding in a bar full of friends and acquaintances. Tonight she is giving me what I want. What I need. Tonight she shows me her strength. Tonight I want to give her one more chance. I lock my eyes on hers. I reach out for the collar, slowly. I dare her with my eyes to let me take it away from her. But she understands what I want. She throws the collar behind her, and it lands on the floor, 10 or 15 feet away. I do not look away from her, but I hear the collar's O-ring hit the floor.

"It's not yours to take anymore, boi."

My eyes well up with tears. I'm angry, yes, but I don't want it to end like this. My eyes flick to where I heard the collar hit the floor. I see someone kick it, accidentally, another few feet away. I know that in a few minutes it will be lost for good. I look directly in front of me at Dani's feet. She is wearing the steel-toed leather boots I've polished so many times. My eyes travel slowly up her black jeans to the bulge in her pants. After four years, I can tell what dick she's wearing through them. She has on her black leather belt tonight too. I remember the night I earned mine with 200 strokes from hers. Her plain white T-shirt covers the tits that even I sometimes forget are there. And then I meet her eyes again. The strength I've longed for these past months is there. I don't think it was ever gone. I think I chose not to see it.

"Please, sir. I'm sorry. My collar—"

"You want it, boi? What makes you think you can wear my

collar now? You've shown me nothing but disrespect for months. You may have earned that collar once, but you've lost it now. If you want it back, you're going to have to do a lot more than just ask."

"Sir…it's going to get lost. It's going to get trampled." My voice is shaking. I can't cry in front of all these people. She knows that. But I'm perilously close.

She nods, then jerks her head in the direction of the collar. "Go find it."

I start to get to my feet, but her hand on the back of my head forces me to my hands and knees.

"Crawl to it, boi. Find it on your hands and knees and bring it to me in your teeth."

"Yes, sir."

I crawl toward the collar, but when I get near it, someone kicks it to my right. I turn to follow it, and someone kicks it past me. I turn around again to see someone's foot planted next to my collar, waiting to kick it again. I look up and see that it's a friend of Dani's. I crawl over, flirtatious smile planted on my lips. I lower my face towards the collar, but Dani's friend kicks it between my legs. What's going on? I look behind me. My collar lies at the feet of another friend of Dani's. Suddenly I realize that this isn't a coincidence. I'm not crawling around randomly. Dani must have talked to these people beforehand. They know what I'm doing, what she's doing to me. But the knowledge doesn't really help.

I follow my collar again, knowing I can't reach it. I'm made to crawl to every corner of the bar, under people's tables, even behind the bar once. Finally someone kicks the collar to Dani. I crawl over, bend down to pick it up, sure that Dani will kick it away again. But she doesn't. The leather feels soft and comfortable, familiar to my teeth. I turn my face up toward Dani to find an evil smirk on her face. She reaches out her open hand, palm up. I drop the collar across her fingers.

"Good boi. Kneel up." The command is one I haven't heard in a while, I obey, rising off my hands, knees together, body perfectly perpendicular to my calves. Once again she dangles the collar inches from my eyes. I fear that she will make me repeat my task, but instead she snaps her wrist upward, catching both ends of my collar in her fist.

"You may have the opportunity to earn this back, boi. Don't take that chance for granted." With those words, she shoves the collar harshly into her front pocket.

I can no longer see it, but the bulge it forms in her pants is unmistakable. I want nothing more than to tear it out of her pocket, put it on, apologize. But she's right. I won't appreciate it, won't respect it, unless I earn it.

I nod slowly. "No, sir. I won't, sir." I'm afraid to make the wrong move, and my fear's effect on my body is unexpected. I feel like a 15-year-old boi, nervous about touching her first girlfriend for fear she'll dump her. I'm shaking, sweating, wet from head to toe. And Dani isn't missing any of it.

"Scared, boi? Afraid I'm going to hurt you? Or afraid I won't? Don't worry, brat, you'll get what's coming to you."

I listen as she orders a rum and coke, wait dutifully while she drinks first one, then a second and orders a third. My knees have become somewhat unaccustomed to kneeling for such a long period of time. It can't have been more than 20, 25 minutes, and they're already aching uncomfortably. I shift my weight to the right and then to the left, thinking Dani is too absorbed in her drinking to notice. I'm wrong. Her backhand is nearly as strong as her forehand. I learned that some time ago, but the slap I'm given for moving without permission reminds me.

"What's the matter, boi? Never could be patient, could you? Or are you suddenly too much of a pussy to kneel for 15 minutes?"

"No, sir. Nothing's wrong, sir."

She takes her time finishing her third drink, then waits to

pay the bartender personally instead of leaving the money on the bar like she always does.

"Heel, boi." She walks towards the door, and I crawl quickly, scrambling to keep up. She walks me out through the front door to her apartment, only a few houses down. I've crawled this route before, but she's impatient tonight, forcing me to crawl almost faster than I am able.

At her door she allows me to stand and follow her inside. I am on my knees again in moments, swaying almost imperceptibly in front of the bulge of her dick. I've never wanted to suck it so bad.

"What do you want, boi?"

"Dick, sir." *Slap.*

"Your dick, sir." *Slap.*

"I want to suck your dick, sir." *Slap.*

"Sir, I want to suck your dick, sir." No slap this time. Damn, she's being a hardass.

She pulls my face forward, allowing me to feel her dick through her jeans. I run my tongue up and down its length, nibble lightly. She's as hard as I am wet.

"Sir, may I take it out, sir?" I look up for my answer, see her nod and unbutton her pants deftly. I pull out her cock. It's my favorite one, the one she had on when we met. It's purple, and the stars that once were indented into its base have long since worn off. It's not too big for my ass, not too small for my cunt. I take it into my mouth slowly, wanting to take my time and savor its taste. She allows me a few minutes to eat it the way I want to, and I feel her getting hotter.

"Want to make me come, boi? You like it when I fuck your face, don't you?" She's starting to grunt now. She grabs the back of my head and pounds in and out of my mouth. "Suck harder, boi. Make me come in your mouth." The head of her dick keeps hitting the back of my mouth. I have to swallow repeatedly to keep from choking. "That's it, boi. Show me how good a cocksucker you are." Her thrusts are getting harder and faster. Her breath is quickening. I know she's close to coming.

"Oh, yeah, boi. I'm gonna come right down your throat, boi. Unhhh…" Her final thrust forces her cock deep into my throat. I can't breathe, but I don't want to anyway. She pulls out and I gasp for breath.

"Not bad, boi. Now, go into my room and kneel by the bed. I'll be there in a minute." I hear her cleaning herself up as I crawl into the bedroom. She has lined up some of our toys on the bed. The cane, three paddles, the strap, the pinwheel.

I stay on my hands and knees until she comes into the room, stands behind me, and tells me to kneel up. She remains out of my line of vision, but I know how she is standing. Straight, with feet slightly apart, hands behind her back. Her favorite stance of power.

"You will receive a punishment tonight that will test the limits of your endurance, boi. However, I have no doubt that you *will* endure it, because at the end of it lies your collar. If you do not wish to be collared, tell me now, and I will not force you to stay." She pauses, giving me a chance to speak. I do not. I cannot. "Good. I will use each of the implements that lie before you. I expect you to count each stroke. Every time you speak, you will address me with respect. You will begin and end each sentence with 'sir.' If you lose count, if you forget to address me, or if you move, I will begin again. Do you understand?"

"Sir, yes, sir."

She starts me off with the lightest paddle. The counting is easy; I receive only 25 strokes. The medium-weight paddle comes next; my ass is beginning to numb. I count to 30, and she stops again. She picks up the heaviest of the paddles. I flinch slightly, knowing I have a hard time not moving when I'm hit with this paddle. Hopefully the numbness will help me. But she doesn't seem to be hitting me. She's waiting for me to regain all feeling! I know I can't stay still in this position.

"Sir, may I kneel forward, sir?"

She takes a moment to think, then says, "You may, pussy boi."

My face flushes. She knows I can't stand being called a pussy. My mouth opens to say something smartassed in response, but I think better of it. I know she's just trying to goad me into more punishment. I bend down, my forehead resting on the triangle formed by my hands, my breasts flattened against my thighs.

"Is that better, pussy?"

I grit my teeth and respond, "Sir, yes, sir."

By now my ass has regained feeling. It's tingling and sore, yet I know it hasn't even begun to hurt.

I bear the first 13 strokes without too much trouble. Then Dani uses more of her strength. I grit my teeth.

"Sir, 14, sir. Sir, 15, sir. Sir, 16, sir." I need to focus my attention on not moving. "Sir, 19, sir." As the paddle comes down again and again, I start to lose track of my count. "Sir, 23, sir?" It's almost a question now.

She hasn't made me start over yet. I must still be right. "Sir, 31, sir." She's hitting me harder and harder. "Sir, 37, sir." My ass is on fire. "Sir, 39, sir." I can't take much more. "Sir, 40, sir."

She stops. My cunt is so wet, I know I must be dripping on the floor.

I see her pick up the strap. It's normally one of my favorite punishments. I love the sound it makes when it hits my ass. The smack of leather on skin. I love the way it feels. The lingering sting, the way you hear the sound first and then a second later the pain comes. But now my ass is tender, I'm not sure I can take it.

The first few strokes bring tears to my eyes. She is spacing the timing just enough to keep me off-guard. *Oh, God.* The tears are coming. Silently, I let them fall down my face. She lets a few more strokes fall on my ass. "Sir, 10, sir." My counting is nearly a whisper. If I were to count louder, she would hear the crying in my voice. "Sir, 11, sir."

The next stroke falls on my upper back. My right shoulder, my left shoulder, my lower back. My ass is grateful for the break.

My tears recede. I'm counting louder now. Almost defiantly. I can take almost anything on my back.

"Sir, 20, sir." I'm almost shouting. I want her to continue. I want to show off my ability to take the strap on the tight skin of my back. "Sir, 26, sir!" I'm getting cocky, counting like an army recruit in his first day of training. Sharp, precise. "Sir, 28, sir!"

The next blow falls on my ass again and knocks all the breath out of me. I was fully unprepared, just as I know she wanted me to be. I can't count. I can't say anything.

"Count, brat. Twenty-nine," she reminds me.

"Sir, 29, sir." It's a squeak, but I've said it. She lands the strap across my ass a few more times, eliciting the same sort of high-pitched response. Then, satisfied that I've lost my cockiness, she moves down to my thighs. She purposefully lets the top of the strap hit my cunt a few times, making me even wetter.

"Sir, 42, sir." I wish that she'd finish and fuck me. I need her cock. I'm moaning quietly between my count now. "Sir, 48, sir."

"Two more, boi."

"Sir, 49, sir." The last blow is on my ass again. "*Sir*, 50, *sir*." I yell it, knowing I'm finished.

"That was good, boi. Are you ready for the cane? Or is that too much for you, pussy boi?"

Oh, God. The cane. I love the cane. I hate the cane. I'm glad she's saved it for last. I know she will make me bleed.

"Sir, I'm ready for it, sir."

She picks up the cane and runs it over my ass a few times. Then she begins. She is very talented with a cane. She starts at the bottom of my ass and works her way upward to the very bottom of my back and then down again. For the first 25 strokes she is in perfect rhythm. Then she begins her pattern of breaking the skin. Three rapid strokes, increasingly hard. The third cuts into me every time. Without out fail, the break makes me suck in my breath so my count comes out, "*FFFFF...* Sir, 28, sir." "*FFFFF...* Sir, 31, sir."

She breaks the skin of my ass, my thighs, my lower back. My head starts to spin. My body is leaking everywhere. Blood, sweat, tears, and come ooze out. I reach 50, 60, 75. My mind has gone completely blank. All it can hold are numbers in succession, and even those seem to come directly from my mouth without any real thought involved.

"Sir, 92, sir." I have left the world and gone to a place where all that exists is me, Dani, and a cane. "Sir, 99, sir. Sir, 100, sir."

And then it is over. Dani picks me up and places me on my stomach on the bed.

"You're a very good boi." Her voice is gentle now, calming me, cradling me. "The collar is almost yours again. I only need to mark you first."

Far away I feel the pinwheel gliding across my back, numbing me. She increases the pressure, now making hundreds of tiny pricks into my back. She wipes the pricks with a cotton ball soaked in alcohol. They feel cool and then sting in a pleasant way.

The blade comes next. I can feel the pressure, but it doesn't hurt at all. The knife is as sharp as a scalpel and just as thin. She covers my upper back with long, diagonal, parallel lines. I feel her sit up and unwrap her tits. She lies on top of me, her breasts against my back. I feel her dick press against my asshole and my cunt. She reaches down to guide it into my cunt and enters me with one stroke. We fuck for only a few minutes before I feel an orgasm aching in me.

"Daddy, may I come?"

"Of course, sweet boi."

Her permission allows my body to explode. I soak her dick and her sheets.

She doesn't pull out but reaches down and pulls my collar out of her pocket. She tightens it around my throat. I am owned again.

About the Contributors

Alice Blue lives in San Francisco. Her work can also be seen in *Anything That Moves* magazine and *The Mammoth Book of New Erotica* (Carroll and Graf).

Rachel Kramer Bussel is a freelance writer living in New York City. She writes the Lusty Lady column for Check This Out! (http://ctomag.com/may16cto/newlust.html), is reviews editor for Venus or Vixen? (http://www.venusorvixen.com), and is an editorial assistant at *On Our Backs*. Her writing has appeared in *Starf*cker* and the *San Francisco Chronicle,* and on CleanSheets.com, NewYorkCitySearch.com, and Lesbianation.com. Visit her Web page at http://raquelita8.tripod.com.

Elise Chapman is an Alabama native and current resident of Texas. She's presently writing essays on sexuality and sex work as well as true-life stories drawn from her experiences working in strip clubs and her adventures in the local leather scene. Her nonacademic writing has appeared in *Danzine,* a quarterly by and for dancers and others who work in the sex industry.

Hilary Cellini Cook is a dyke lawyer lady with hammer-swinging, child-carrying biceps. She is a good girl Canadian who survived six years of forced relocation to California. Fleeing a too sunny (her complexion is sexier in colder climates), too military (she liked the uniforms but not the attitude) climate, she now lives back in Toronto with her two children, four computers, and the young butch girlfriend she abducted from San Diego.

DeLaine, a native of Hillside, N.J., recently relocated to Los Angeles with her partner of three years. She has been writing erotica since the 10th grade. She looks forward to publishing more stories in the near future and hopes to release a novel in fall 2001. DeLaine would like to dedicate "Peaches and Orchids," her first published story, to D. Dove, with love through thick and thicker.

Beth Greenwood hails from the Southwest. This is her first published story.

Lynne Herr spends her idle hours working up the courage to wear the flamboyant shoes she bought in Korea. The rest of the time she freelances.

Karleen Pendleton Jimenez is a Chicana boy dyke currently residing in Canada. Originally from Los Angeles, she is a writer and teacher. She was formerly the director of Queer Players, a creative writing and performance group in San Diego, and currently works with Joint Effort in Toronto, a group of women cultural workers bringing creative workshops to women in prison.

Jianda Johnson lives in Southern California. A freelance writer, she is also a singer, musician, and filmmaker. On and offline her fiction, nonfiction, and poetry have been published in *Clean Sheets, Doorknobs, Bodypaint, ChickClick*, the University of California, Irvine's *Faultline, Womyn's Quarterly,* the anthology *Well-Rounded* (Cleis Press), and on About.com. Her home page can be found at http://www.soul.about.com.

Louise Kington still can't believe her luck in stumbling upon such an amazing maybe–dyke at a sleazy strip club, and she continues to fantasize about her.

Rosalind Christine Lloyd is captivated by the aesthetic and limitless use of the imagination through erotica and contemporary fiction. Her work has been featured in several anthologies, including *Hot & Bothered II, Pillow Talk II, Set in Stone, Best American Erotica 2001,* and other various gay and lesbian publications. Currently the travel editor for *Venus* magazine, this native New Yorker–Harlem resident–lesbian of color is working on her first novel.

Meghan Maury lives in western Massachusetts with her partner. She works at a bookstore and spends all her spare time reading and writing.

Kristen E. Porter is an acupuncturist and the Clinic Director of the AIDS Care Project in Boston. She has previously been published in *Philogyny* magazine and the anthology *Skin Deep.* She is a community activist and lesbian–event producer, and each week she hosts host dyke night at the Midway Café. She lives in the Jamaica Plain section of Boston with the love of her life and is looking forward to their first pregnancy.

Julia Price lives in Los Angeles with her lover. "Piss Off!" is her first published erotic story.

Rebecca Rajswasser, a former schoolteacher, lives and works in New York City. Her work can be seen in *Chicago Free Press* and the anthology *Fusion* as well as in the upcoming We'Moon 2002 calendar journal. When not "researching" and writing erotica, Rebecca spends her time riding the subway looking for the meaning of life. Rebecca would like to thank Holli Hamilton, who made this story possible.

When **Tammy Stoner** sleeps she dreams about tap-dancing pugs and humorless tapeworms playing blackjack in her colon. When she's awake she writes about it. She's just finished her first novel, *Fish Orchard*.

Tristan Taormino is the author of *The Ultimate Guide to Anal Sex for Women* and director and star of the video of the same name. She is series editor of *Best Lesbian Erotica,* editor of *On Our Backs* (where the article "I Was A Pro-Dom Virgin" originally appeared), a columnist for *The Village Voice,* and sex-advice columnist for *Taboo magazine.* She is also the queen of her virtual world, www.puckerup.com. Her new book on sex will be published by Regan Books in 2001.

Violet Taylor is a native Angeleno who really does live in West Hollywood, Calif., with her lover, who may or may not be named Jordan—but then, don't they always change the names to protect the innocent?

RandenTrashinaCann is a writer, producer, choreographer, and performance artist. She can usually be found sleazing in dark alleys, parking lots, or smelly bathrooms looking for a hot fagdyke time.

Alma Vada is a trial attorney who has published in Salon.com, *Traveler's Tales: Paris*, *California Lawyer* magazine, and *Tokyo Family Law Journal*. She is working on a collection of stories about her adventures in Thailand, Irian Jaya, Nepal, Australia, and Sumatra. She lives in Northern California with her partner, who is an Episcopal minister.

Sarah b Wiseman endures the extreme weather of southeastern Ontario. She loves the feeling of snowflakes falling on bare nipples. Her work has appeared in various Canadian journals and is forthcoming in *Fusion*, a photo book on alternative sexuality.